Phantom Drift Limited
La Grande, Oregon

Issue One
Fall, 2011

Phantom Drift
A Journal of New Fabulism

Editorial Board
    David Memmott, Managing Editor
    Leslie What, Fiction Editor
    Matt Schumacher, Poetry Editor

Accounts & Subscriptions
    Sue Hoyt

Cover Design & Design Consultant
    Kristin Summers, redbat design

Issue One Cover Art
    Jessica Plattner

Phantom Drift is a literary journal dedicated to building an understanding of and appreciation for New Fabulism and a Literature of the Fantastic. The journal will be published annually in the fall of each year. The first issue was made possible by a grant of support from Wordcraft of Oregon, LLC. Phantom Drift Limited is a non-profit organization and donations are deductible to the extent allowed by law. Readers can subscribe for $15.00 (postage paid) on the *Phantom Drift* website hosted by Wordcraft of Oregon:
http://www.wordcraftoforegon.com/pd.html

Or subscriptions can be ordered by direct mail by sending check or money order for $15.00 to:
Phantom Drift
c/o Wordcraft of Oregon, LLC
PO Box 3235
La Grande, OR 97850

Phantom Drift accepts submissions from December 1 – March 31. For submission guidelines and electronic submission, please see our website.

Copyright 2011, Phantom Drift Limited. Copyrights to text, poems and artwork in this issue are held by the individual creators. No material may be reprinted without permission of the journal or artists.

ISSN: 2162-8211
ISBN: 978-1-877655-73-9

PHANTOM CROSSING: EDITORIAL

In a brief article for the anthology, *The Highest State of Consciousness*, edited by John White (Anchor Books, 1972), Stanley Krippner identifies twenty states of consciousness: dreaming state, sleeping state, hypnagogic state, hypnopompic state, hyperalert state, lethargic state, states of rapture, states of hysteria, states of fragmentation, regressive states, meditative states, trance states, reverie, daydreaming state, internal scanning, stupor, stored memory, "expanded" consciousness states and "normal" everyday waking state. Each of these states identified by Krippner could be differentiated subjectively by percipients and often objectively measured by observers. Each state has its own distinct attributes and resulting behaviors, some endearing, some antisocial, some downright intimidating. The point of this is though different from our "normal," psychological functioning, many of these states occur at some point in the course of our lifetimes, a number of them in the course of a 24-hour period, flowing seamlessly from one into another without calling a lot of attention to the transitions. They are as much a part of our lives as the "normal" state but unfortunately marginalized by prevailing social and scientific paradigms, political correctness and fear of the unknown. In different cultures, these non-ordinary states are respected, honored, sometimes even sought out to introduce an individual to an experience of wholeness, or what Williams James called an activation of the unconscious. To my mind, this sounds a lot like the current state of publishing in America—with the mainstream commercial market dominating much like the "waking state" while all else is driven to the fringes. This is not a healthy state of affairs.

Phantom Drift exists in a zone of intersection where opposites become entangled, where the greyness of possibility defeats easy separation of black and white, heaven and earth, spirit and flesh, dream and reality, science and religion, conscious and unconscious. Furthermore, this blurring or overlapping of opposites can symbolize a process of healing and awakening. As one long fascinated with the implications of quantum physics, I find cross-genre, fabulist fiction to be delightfully subversive because it exists in a state of quantum uncertainty like Shrödinger's Cat—difficult to label, impossible to nail down, both wave and particle at the same time.

Each issue/volume of *Phantom Drift* will be another installment in an editorial aim of resisting the temptation to "tell" the creative community what we mean by "new fabulism" or a "literature of the fantastic" by instead "showing" you. Our editors are acutely attuned to a mission of exploring and supporting a range of work that may well be indescribable.

Yet their backgrounds prepare them to "know it when they see it," recognizing work that reaches into the unknown, touching something invisible, wading into swift current like St. Christopher in our cover art by Jessica Plattner, carrying our child-self across the river.

Whether it's *The Wizard of Oz* or *Alice Through the Looking Glass,* an apple tree that throws it's apples in anger or a cat that vanishes leaving it's grin floating in thin air, fabulist writers have the uncanny ability to transport us to the edge of a cosmic whirlpool called mystery. *Perfect conditions for magical thinking.*

In 1987, I started a small journal, *Ice River Magazine*, to explore, for lack of a better description, a literature of the fantastic. A literature of curious cross-fertilizations. A literature of intersections. Literary science fiction. Modern fantasy. Magic realism. Surrealism. Fabulist tales of inner worlds outside of time. Political satire. Techo-altered landscapes..

When Bruce Sterling published what critics refer to as his "seminal essay" on Slipstream, he referred to "a remarkable interview with Carter Scholz" published in *New Pathways* 11, July 1988. That interview was conducted by Misha Nogha, fiction editor/contributing editor for *New Pathways*. Misha's *Prayers of Steel* would ultimately become the first book published by my small press, Wordcraft of Oregon, in it's Speculative Writers Series in 1988. In the same issue as Sterling's essay on Slipstream was an essay by John Shirley, "Beyond Cyberpunk: The New Science Fiction Underground" in which Shirley listed several authors published by *Ice River* and mentioned the magazine as one of the small magazines publishing some of the best new fiction. A loose consortium of magazines/presses, i.e. *New Pathways*, *Science Fiction Eye* and *Back Brain Recluse* (BBR-England) were exploring desktop publishing and drawing upon many of the same authors.

Authors discovered through *Ice River* sustained my publishing interest for at least a decade. One thing that hasn't changed in that time is the fact that there are both commercially-successful writers whose more challenging narratives are largely ignored by commercial markets and acclaimed literary writers whose work has never found a commercial audience. I hope the pages of *Phantom Drift* brings them together to stir up a little karma. With the convergence of two fine editors, Leslie What in fiction and Matt Schumacher in poetry, whether or not we recapture that same energy, I trust *Phantom Drift* will create its own.

David Memmott, Managing Editor
July 25, 2011

Table of Contents

Editorial

❖ FICTION

Ray Vukcevich 7
Eliot Fintushel 11
David Eric Tomlinson 32
Peter Grandbois 65
Carolyn Ives Gilman 73
Daniel Grandbois 87
Nisi Shawl 91
Brian Evenson 116
Joe L. Murr 120
Geronimo G. Tagatac 129
Stefanie Freele 147

◉ POETRY

Aaron Anstett 10
Joshua McKinney 30
Wade German 49
Anita Sullivan 74
Richard Crow 90
Stephen McNally 123
Jonathan Ball 145
Lawrence Raab 151

NON-FICTION/FEATURES

Thomas E. Kennedy 17
Jessica Plattner/Jodi Varon 50
Matt Schumacher 76
Richard Schindler/Michael Chocholak 99

Contributor Notes 154

# Ray Vukcevich
The Problem of Furniture

Everyone in the room has mixed feelings. Jane and Marcie on the couch, David and Pablo at the door. The situation is a perfect introduction to the Problem of Furniture.

Some background first.

It's not entirely true that we are all multiple personalities. Oh, why beat around the bush with nuance? Actually, that is exactly the case. All of us house at least two and sometimes more than two people in our heads. We suppose it's possible there are people who only have one, rare cases, tragic cases, cases not covered in this report but only mentioned here to avoid confusion. Sometimes people do become aware of their neighbors, and this is thought to be a sad mental illness, but most people remain utterly unaware of their mental roommates. The sad cases can be tricky. If a person is suffering from a mental disorder, not all of the other people in the head are suffering from it, too. Generally speaking, a "person" in a given head is aware of only about 10 percent of what the brain is doing. Other people can be using some of the other parts, and there can be sharing. Being aware of a part of the brain does not mean being aware that someone else is also aware of that part.

Most often the people in a given head are very similar to one another, brothers and sisters, really. If you could meet the siblings in your head, you would probably not think they were much alike, because you would be noticing all the differences, but someone in an entirely different head would right away see how alike you all were. No two of us were raised by the same parents, however. Or at least, that is very rare. There is always room for strange occurrences like the unfortunate situation where a parent simply can't see the child or vice versa.

This similarity of personalities greatly simplifies the problem of stuff. It doesn't eliminate it altogether. If that were true, there would be no so-called "Problem of Furniture" and this report would be about something else.

The Problem of Furniture is simply this. One of you, Jane, for example, might love that oxblood leather couch, and Marcie might be thinking she wouldn't be caught dead with such an ugly thing in her living room — it looks like a crouching masked wrestler or a bulldog, and it's made out of cows! So, the one who likes the couch buys it (with her totally separate checking account in a store that Marcie would never set foot in) and puts it right over there beneath the big windows, and Marcie forever after carefully steps around it and never notices it. She who loves it, dusts it and sweeps under it and lounges upon it, and even once got herself fed grapes while gazing into nearly violet eyes and will forever remember the image while the other one will be strangely puzzled and uneasy about why she never gets right up next to the big windows anymore even on the coldest days when she would like to put her nose against the glass and remember her childhood.

This explains why so many people have too much stuff.

But we should clear up the question, we know you're wondering, some of you will have guessed, of who "we" who are writing this report are. We are, of course, space aliens. (But to be fair and comprehensive, we are also you, since brain blending means things are not always so cut and dry.)

We are always looking out of the eyes and watching everything you do. Sometimes we interfere just because we can. Some of you think we are gods. Many of you think we are only one god, which is a laugh since we are so many. Those of you who become aware of us often give us names with no vowels, and you hear our names as the sound of breaking glass (David and Pablo) or the deep inside sound a cat makes when it's about to go from profoundly sad to irrationally happy (Marcie and Jane).

And how can it be that you are reading this report? Somehow one of you has invaded our invisible orbiting base, learned our language, stolen these pages, translated our words into one of your human languages, and now you are reading them! Maybe you wore a rubber suit with the extra limbs and things. It couldn't have been easy keeping the skin so moist and glistening. I bet you wore something provocative so we would only give you sidelong glances and only notice certain parts and not even see the other more difficult areas moving like monkeys, all elbows and knees, in a rubber sack.

What a blunder on our part! Isn't that just like us? This is the way the cat always gets out of the bag.

"That's ridiculous," Jane says.

Or maybe it was Marcie.

No, probably Jane, since she's sitting on the couch, and she looks so hard and hurt, you break my heart, but you can go to hell.

We could have told you the "We Are Really All Aliens" routine would not work in this situation. If you are going to get out the door in one piece, you are simply going to have to make a break for it.

David is vaguely aware that the other guy in his head really does love the other woman in Jane's head. It's like she said the other day, someone in you is looking right past someone in me. Now he knows what she meant, sort of, but it's probably too late.

Come on, man, Pablo pleads with David, you can't do this to me!

Meanwhile Marcie is thinking hey! Hey! Where did this awful couch come from? And why am I lounging on it? And where is Pablo going looking so conflicted?

Sit up!

"Pablo?" Marcie holds out her hands. Come to me, please, come to me.

Pablo walks us across the room to the couch and sits us down beside her.

We are suddenly so shy with one another.

But all twenty of our fingers know what to do, and soon we are naked on the cool smooth leather and later we wonder if that was the storm and had it passed now? Was everything okay?

She's kneeling now on the couch. Come on, she says, and he gets up beside her.

Let's put our noses against the cold glass.

We do that.

Isn't this nice?

Her voice is so strange and pinched.

It really is nice, we say, echoing. Oh, look, your old pink bicycle.

Let's forever freeze just like this.

Whatever you do, dear Alien Overlords, don't beam us up now.

 Aaron Anstett

Good Morning

Fifty-some years after the war, a kamikaze lands in my yard,
gently, like a sheet of newsprint.

"Ohayo gozaimasu," I say, though it is evening, light grown ochre
and pink, day disappearing across the Zero's wings.

He shinnies from the cockpit, the thinnest man I've seen.
He has evaded the radar. He's fallen

for decades, believing he'll attack
the coast of America, setting all the pines in Oregon blazing.

I take him inside, where he drinks a glass of water.
It is clear. It tastes nothing like the ocean.

(originally appeared in *No Accident*, Backwaters Press)

Eliot Fintushel
NO, REALLY

How's everybody feeling tonight? Pretty good? Great! Great!

I want to thank each and every one of you for braving the lead rain and the gummyclouds to make it here tonight to Jake's Yok Spot, the one and only boss-certified human rec facility in the city and county of 27-E3. I'm Jackie Jock the Joke Man. I love you to pieces, folks, and I'm here to make you laugh your teeth right back into your gums.

Any butlers in the audience? None of you had to bring your butlers, right? Because I have a little gripe with butlers, and I'd like to feel that I can speak freely here. Oh, I mean, it's no big deal. I mean, hey, nobody loves butlers more than I do, loves the whole institution of butlers more than I do.

You hear that, boss? I LOVE 'EM TO FRIGGING DEATH!

Just kidding there. No, really. Status quo is the way to go. I love everything nowadays. No, really.

But don't you just hate it when they make you take them along? Even if you love your butler to frigging death, which is exactly my mind state, believe you me, still, for us humans—no offence, boss—but, for us humans, it can cramp your style. Know what I'm talking about? I mean, love them as we do, butlers are not always perfectly sympatico.

Like, for example, you know how when you wake up in the morning and there's this, you know, this *thing* all over your tongue? And you, like, go to the bathroom to get the butler to hose it down—I mean, with his hose, right? Hey, don't laugh--you do it too. You have the frigging butler hose it down for you. What, am I being uncivilized to mention this? This is life in this day and age. Deal with it—am I right?

Okay, so you get him to hose it down—like I said. And the son of a bitch is gonna have an attitude. You know he's gonna have an attitude. Am I right? Are you with me? Because he's in with the bosses. All the damn butlers are in with the bosses. What are we to them, right? Like, "Maybe I'll hose it off of you and maybe I won't" kind of thing. You see what I'm saying?

So you have to shoot him.

No, really. Take it easy, folks. Thanks for the rim shot, Sal. Without the damn rim shot, who'd know when to laugh, am I right?

Okay, relax, guys. Just joking up here. Nobody's shooting anybody. Nobody can get the draw on a butler, anyway. Everybody knows that. I'm just having a good time up here. Everybody, relax.

So anyway, I had this butler with a real attitude, you know. I mean he had an attitude the size of the bosses' goddam mothership. He had an attitude the size of their goddam grandmothership, for Christ's sakes. He wouldn't so much as let me get near him if I had a *thing* on my tongue. And there I am, down on my knees, hands in my jammies, a *thing* on my tongue, begging the goddam butler for a hose-off, and he won't let me near him. So what can you do?

Because you can't exactly fire *a butler, can you?*

I know, I know. You can stop all the groaning now--I know that's an old one. "You can't exactly *fire* a butler": I know that one came in with test tube babies. I was just putting you on.

So I was saying, I get up in the morning, there's this *thing* all over my tongue. I know you've all experienced this. You all know the drill. You've all read the bumf. Next step: get it hosed down. You've got to, am I right? Otherwise, it swallows you from inside out. Two, three days, and you look like a beached, rotted boss—oops! Did I say beached rotted boss? I meant beached rotted fish. Fish, that's right. So you've got to get the *thing* hosed.

Problem is, like I said, I've got this butler who has to play the shrinking violet whenever I approach him with a *thing* on my tongue. No stomach for it. You know the type. So what am I supposed to do?

You ever try going to work with a *thing* all over your tongue? Try it sometime. You know you can't. The bosses will kill it before you pass through the iris, and bosses ain't butlers, baby; they cultivate no subtlety. When the *thing* fries, you fry with it. What do they care from humans, am I right? I can tell that you know what I mean.

But, hey, I mean no offense to the bosses. After all, what would we have without them? The mind reels. Food, shelter, personal integrity . . . No really. Just kidding. Nobody could stand that much happiness. No, just kidding. I love the bosses. Everybody human's gotta love the bosses . . . or else.

No, really. The bosses have their responsibilities, after all. Let's hear it for the bosses. Yes, and for the workholes, too. You know you love them. It's like night down there twenty-four seven. Night and winter and drought. Who wouldn't love them? No, really. I mean, okay, so it's maybe a little unpleasant, the sores and the gradual loss of little things like hair, sexual potency, bowel control, your mind . . .

Just kidding. Just kidding. Thanks for the rim shot, Sal. I want everybody to know I'm just kidding up here.

No, really. Come on, you know in your heart you wouldn't go back to the old way if they gave you your gonads back double-bagged and with an extra ball. I mean, think of all the good we're doing down there. I don't know about you, but I find a deep satisfaction in knowing that my labor is serving to make others happy, and the fact that they're three hundred light years away and don't know who or even what I am, hey, that just makes my satisfaction the purer. Friends, it is better to give than to receive.

So, where was I? Oh yeah, so here I am sitting up in bed with the *thing* wrapped around my tongue, as will happen, and my butler is playing hard-to-get. He's in the bathroom checking out the drainpipes.

Wait a minute. Wait a minute. Drainpipes. Don't get me started. Do you--now you youngsters bear with me on this, because this is a Meaningful Moment for us old farts here—do you remember when a drainpipe was a frigging drainpipe? Huh? Do you? When water went down it? And sewage? And, like, feces and so on? You tell me now, was that a time? Wasn't it? You saw what was coming out of you, for Christ's sake. I mean, the only thing that came out of you was the dregs of what you'd put in. I mean, there's an elegance to that, am I right? No, seriously. In the old days, the *human* days, you knew what was in your goddam drainpipe.

But these modern drainpipes, the ones the butlers are always checking, the ones they put them there to check, only the bosses ever know what's in them—the bosses and the butlers, of course. And, hey, if you don't like it, *try firing a butler!*

I know, I know. It's that old chestnut again. I'm just putting you on, folks. You gotta keep up here. I'm just joshing up here. Hey, those ancient drainpipes are nothing to the ones we have today, the ones the bosses gave us. I mean, try to read a person's thoughts from the old-fashioned drainpipes, huh? All you got is half-digested broccoli, maybe, a couple of spent condoms, and a load of sugary pee. What can you read off of that, am I right?

Whereas, your modern drainpipes, the ones the bosses are all the time poring over, if you'll excuse a little pun, they reveal everything. Everything. Everything plus. Okay, everybody, put your right pinky in your brainhole, right where the nightdrain hooks up—that's right, jimmy the plug and stick in your pinky. This is what I call the Toiletworld salute. Now repeat after me: I LOVE THE BOSSES.

Okay, plug up now.

Where was I? Drainpipes. Butlers. Oh yeah, the *thing* on my tongue. The butler's checking out my thought processes in the bathroom. He doesn't want to know about any *thing* on my tongue, this butler. He's dumb as shit. They're all of them dumb as shit, you know it and I know it. Why would the bosses waste brainpower on a thing like a butler, a mere functionary, a chaperone, if you will, a personal attendant, a flunky, a thug? No, just kidding there. Hell, I never met a butler I didn't like.

But the fact is they're dumb as shit. Now, some humans feel insulted by the fact that the bosses seem to feel that butlers occupy a higher station than humans, that butlers are allowed more freedom and given swifter audience and greater trust and praise and everything laudable and desirable, more of everything than us humans. Some humans just don't get it.

No, really. They don't understand how much greater and wiser and nobler the bosses are than us benighted humans and how grateful we ought to be for the work they give us and for every word that cometh from their mouths—if you can call those bloody ichor-dripping chitinous black maws of theirs "mouths"—how grateful for the butlers they have vouchsafed unto us for ever and ever and let the people say (This is your cue, folks...): Amen.

So, anyway, I love my goddam butler, yes I do, but I have to get this goddam *thing* off my tongue, and I'm stuck with this son of a bitch of a butler who won't have any part of it. He won't let me near his goddam electron hose. Of course, the bosses wouldn't trust one of us humans with an electron hose. No way. Hell, they'd have to be dumber than shit themselves to do that. They'd have to be frigging suicidal, am I right?

No, seriously. They know what we'd do with one of their frigging electron hoses, if we ever got hold of one. Hell, we'd blow them off the frigging planet, wouldn't we? Right back to wherever the goddam hell they came from, wouldn't we?

I said, wouldn't we?

I didn't hear you.

Right. I heard you that time. Maybe *they* even heard you. Better do another little Toiletworld salute. Pinkies ready? Brainholes ready?

I LOVE THE BOSSES.

Okay. Just so that's clear. You know, before the goddam bosses—and I use the term "goddam" affectionately, of course—before the goddam bosses hit the scene, nobody Earthside had even heard of your *things* on the tongue. I just want to make that point, folks. Point of record: pre-boss, no *things* on the tongue. It's their parasite, not ours. Like spikegrass and gummyclouds and your goddam what-they-call "lead rain." Those little pleasantnesses came along with the bosses, you know.

What's the matter, Buster? Ain't I funny enough for you? Jake, freshen up this guy's needle—on me; I ain't funny enough for the gentleman. In fact, freshen up mine. Yes, again, damn you. Freshen up mine. I need it. We all need it. Don't we need it, folks? How about a little support here to make Jake freshen my needle, a little cheer for your favorite funnyman, huh?

Thank you, thank you, everybody. And thank you, Jake. No, really. What? I'm not going to offend anybody, Jake. Take it easy. You're not going to lose any goddam license.

So, like I was saying, these tongue wrapping *things* we got now, they belonged to the bosses, like barnacles to a ship, see? But the *things* liked us better—this is what I read in *Scientific World*, so you know it's gotta be true. I mean frigging *Scientific World* doesn't have a butler. Not yet. So you can trust it, is what I'm saying. It hasn't been muzzled, see?

Not like me. Oh, yes. I've been muzzled. I've been butlered. I've been *thinged*. I love my bosses. I slave every day in the workholes, don't I, and I hardly remember what it is to make love to a woman--you youngsters, simmer down there, because we old guys are having us another goddam Moment, if you please—to make love, dammit, love. Remember goddam love? Before they butlered the bejeezus out of us and set us to work mining our own God-given earth and our own nervous systems, for Christ's sakes, to ship off and feed wherever the hell it is those miscreant alien sons of bitches call home? Remember love? You youngsters, you no-navel youngsters, you poor test tube baby generation, you don't know shit about frigging love, do you?

Jake, if you wave that thing in my face once more, as God is my witness, I'll bite your nose off and spit it down your throat. No, really, folks, Jake is a great fellow. Let's hear it for Jake. Let's hear it for all the collaborationist boss-licking sons of bitches. Hip hip hurray!

So, where was I? Oh yeah, in bed with a *thing* around my tongue and a butler in the bathroom, sifting through the goddam drainpipe and prickling like a porcupine at the smell of my regard. Oh yes, they can smell you regarding them, can't they? But do I give a good goddam? Say it with me, folks:

NO!

No, I do not give a good goddam. I'm tired to death of hosting their *things* on my tongue and working their goddam workholes and offering my nervous system up to their mining operations and every other goddam indignity they've visited on us and, you know what? Here's what: as I sit there with a tongue full of *thing* and a goddam recalcitrant butler, I begin to think that they *can* be fired. I march right in on the lazy-assed mofo—somebody rip that cell phone out of Jake's paw, would you?—I march right in, see, because I don't give a damn anymore.

There he is, this butler of mine, bristling with pore-embedded microblasters all bared and armed and ready to roll, all pointing at Yours Truly like the frigging Sierra Nevadas seen from a plane, and I stand there cool as a dead man's cravat, and I say, "Listen, Jeeves, do you think I could use your hose for a second to wash this little *thing* off my tongue? Do you think the bosses would mind?"

Somebody lock the door, would you? There seems to be somebody there, and I don't think they can afford the cover. That's right. Just lean a chair against it for now. We're having a private little Moment, aren't we? Let them just siren and bullhorn out there for a while. Hell, it'll do them good for a change. Life has become so goddam boring, don't you agree?

So I say, "Jeeves," I say, "would you mind?" And he is dumbfounded. He has no response programmed for this particular little finesse. The bosses have no goddam sense of humor, have they? They have no understanding of the sheer power of human goddam perversity. So Jeeves is sitting there over the drainpipe, like a stunned mullet, and I just reach down for his hose.

"Jeeves," I say, "you're fired." And I hose him. All that's left of him is the smell. And then I hose the *thing* off my tongue.

Let them break the goddam door, brothers. I'm packing heat. And you've been lied to.

Butlers *can* be fired.

 Thomas E. Kennedy
REALISM & OTHER ILLUSIONS

"If you want to give a natural appearance to an imaginary creature, a dragon for example, use the head of a mastiff or a pointer, the eyes of a cat, the ears of a hedgehog, the snout of a hare, the smile of a lion, the temples of a cock, and the neck of a tortoise."
    -Leonardo da Vinci

"If people see a lion, they run away; if they only apprehend a deduction, they keep wandering round in an experimental humor. Now how is the poet to convince like nature, and not like books?"
    -Robert Louis Stevenson

When we read a piece of fiction, what is it about the work that inspires the "willing suspension of disbelief" that Coleridge identified as necessary to the experience of literature? What makes us willing, even eager to believe that the artificial world into which the writer invites us is a real one? The problem may not be so acute with realistic works — if we pick up a book and begin to read, for example,

> "The Jackman's marriage had been adulterous and violent, but in its last days, they became a couple again, as they might have if one of them were slowly dying..."

we accept the premise immediately. With this opening to his story, "The Winter Father," Andre Dubus fills us in on the essence of a compelling situation which we automatically place in a setting in the real world, and he goes on to tell skillfully a moving story about the dissolution of family life which is or was so central to the short story of the eighties and nineties.

Likewise, we react with belief when we read the opening of Raymond Carver's "Collectors."

> "I was out of work. But any day I expected to hear from up north. I lay on the sofa and listened to the rain. Now and then I'd lift up and look through the curtain for the mailman."

The scene is not unfamiliar. It is set with objects familiar to us, simple actions that we know from our own experience, charged subtly with emotions that we ourselves have experienced or could easily imagine experiencing.

Gladys Swan opens her novel *Carnival for the Gods* like this:

> "It was the first time Dusty had ever backhanded her, and it was not just the blow, the pain, the blood from her lip flowing saltily into her mouth that gave Alta the shock: it was the sense that something fatal had struck at the roots of her life."

Again, a situation sufficiently grounded in recognizably real detail to be accepted without trouble as reality, as is this opening of Francois Camoin's story, "Lieberman's Father":

> "Lieberman had his eyes on his chicken salad and so at first didn't see the woman. She stopped short at his table and stood swaying a little this way and that, looking like a person who has just bumped into something and is wondering if she's hurt herself."

Such openings seem immediately real enough, "normal" enough not to raise questions in our minds about where they are happening. They seem to be happening in the same world we occupy, and we accept them as such. But sometimes they seem to nudge toward the border of another dimension. Here's how Gordon Weaver's "The Interpreter" starts:

> "It is as if... It is as if I cannot remember the things I must say to myself. It is as if all the words I know in both English and my native Mandarin have fled from me, evaporated into the cold, misty air of this wretched place, into the wet fogs that greet us each morning... It is as if each bitter day is the first and I wake chilled...knowing nothing until I can remember some words, something to say to myself that will allow me to rise."

Not *un*realistic, yet there is an edge of the other there that makes us a little unsure just where we are.

And what is one to make of a short story from *Leaf Storm* by Gabriel Garcia Márquez that opens with a character named Palayo walking home from the beach, entering his courtyard to find "a very old man, lying face down in the mud" and unable to rise because "his enormous wings" are in the way? How are we to suspend our disbelief and enter

Márquez's world — even if we desperately want to?

Or the opening of Robert Coover's story "Beginnings":

"In order to get started, he went to live alone on an island and shot himself. His blood, unable to resist a final joke, splattered the cabin wall in a pattern that read: It is important to begin when everything is already over."

How are we to be encouraged or enabled to incorporate the conditions of that bizarre world into our own experience?

All of the examples given above can be grouped into two different categories which differ from each other in one basic manner of narrative strategy. The first five examples (Dubus, Carver, Swan, Camoin, Weaver) being in more or less clear "realistic" modes, invite us into a world which from the start presents itself as part of the world we automatically would assume to be the setting of any occurrence related to us, be it fiction or nonfiction. The setting, we assume, is *our* world, *here*, where we live, or at least in some other land that really exists and can be "seen" in the atlas. With Weaver, we are a little uncertain where we are, and with an opening like Márquez's or Coover's, we know that the setting is not a "real" one, that the "place" in which the story occurs would seem rather to be located somewhere in the imagination than in the external world.

How, then, is the writer to persuade us of the "reality" of what he is reporting in a manner as though it is really occurring or has occurred? How does the author succeed in making us read on, in suspending our disbelief?

It is important to recognize that all of the above examples are examples of illusion, whether the illusion is a realistic one, a surrealistic one, a superrealistic one, or a so-called fabulist, metafictional, or postmodern one. It was the French novelist Émile Zola who said, "The realists of art should really be called the illusionists." Or as Robert Louis Stevenson put it over a hundred years ago, in a review of Walt Whitman's *Leaves of Grass*: "This question of realism, let it be then clearly understood, regards not in the least degree the fundamental truth, but only the technical method of a work of art."

While the overall technique or strategy may vary, the basic trick, the basic illusion, is generally pretty much the same, what is called verisimilitude — from the Latin *verisimilitudo* — or *verus similis* — *verus* (true) and *similis* (similar), or the French *vrai semblance* —- that is, something which has the appearance of being true or real, something which *seems* to be true or plausible or likely. Some theorists, like John Gardner, hold the use of verisimilitude to mean that the writer evokes in a large sense, a "true likeness" of the world in which we live — which harkens back to Aristotle's mimetic theory of art put forth in his *Poetics*, that art imitates or mirrors life — but this seems to me too narrow a view of the concept and, ultimately, one that cannot hold, for *no* writer of fiction, not even the most realistic, not even the superrealists, the Edward Hoppers or Duane Hansens or Kurt Trampedachs of prose, fashions a "true likeness" of the world in the largest sense. Have you ever noticed that in Hopper's wonderful evocative portraits of the city there is never any rubbish in the street? All manner of distortion, selection, rearrangement of facts and details is necessary in the writing of fiction. Therefore, I hold to the interpretation of the concept of verisimilitude as merely the creation of an imaginary universe which seems to be real, and that all writers of fiction seek to create an imaginary universe which seems to be real via the use, either continual or occasional, of verisimilitude.

What is verisimilitude? My definition is this: Verisimilitude is that quality of a work of fiction by which a physical, psychological, and spiritual reality is rendered such that the reader is persuaded to suspend disbelief in order that the author's creative discovery regarding existence may be explored and experienced by the reader.

How can this concept apply to the last two examples given above? Márquez and Coover? How can such pieces be given the appearance of reality, most specifically of a physical reality?

As Flannery O'Connor says, "Fiction begins where human knowledge begins — with the senses." We have only five ways of perceiving reality: we can see it, hear it, taste it, smell it, touch it. Or in the case of fiction, we can *seem* to do these things.

Let's look at how Marquez does this with the old man with wings. How does he make us believe in this? First of all, he is lying in the mud, about as vivid and clearly grounded an image as can be found. If he appeared flying above Palayo's head, or seated on a cloud with a harp and wearing immaculate white linen, our doubt might be so much stronger, but when we see the mud on the old angel's face, he has been brought down to earth and our senses begin to respond, our perception of our senses, and as we read on we learn that this old man has very few teeth in his mouth and that "his huge buzzard wings" are "dirty and half-plucked." As we get even closer, we learn further that the old angel has "an unbearable smell," and that the backs of his wings are infested with lice! This Márquez, we begin to feel, he knows his angels! By now the reader has seen and smelled this creature and has shivered at the sight of the lice chewing at the spotty pink chicken flesh of his wings, and this preposterous bizarre creature has been admitted into our imagination by Gárcia's brilliant use of verisimilitude — the replica of that which our senses can perceive, even if only the imaginary counterparts of our senses perceiving the imagined aspects of an image.

Thus, Márquez has shocked us out of our normal expectations of reality, only to coax us back in again by manipulating our senses, turning them against our skepticism. We are made to *smell* the universe being painted in the sky for us. How can you deny the existence of something that *stinks*? "Creations of the mind," Baudelaire said, "are more alive than matter."

Interestingly, though, if we look further at some of the so-called "realistic" examples given above — let's pick Camoin and Swan — we will find a strategy which is very much the reverse of that used by the Márquez example given.

In the Camoin story, we follow a half page of fairly ordinary realistic description. The woman speaks to the man at the table, addresses him by his name. He does not recognize her, asks how she could know his name, and she tells him he'll have to prepare himself for a shock. "This won't be easy for you," she says. She asks permission to sit down, to drink a glass of water, and then she tells him, "I am your father."

He answers, "I already have a father," and she says, "I am your real father." And the remainder of this realistic story deals with the main character dealing with this incomprehensible, impossible, unreal, paradoxical, yet somehow intriguing, compelling situation of a man being accosted by a woman who claims to be his real father. Camoin snares us in a realistic trap into following an impossible situation in which he creates a reality that defies the natural laws — or at the very least the terminology — we have come to know and trust in our own "real" world. Bertold Brecht: "Art is not a mirror held up to reality, but a hammer with which to shape it."

Similarly, Gladys Swan's realistic story begins with something about as real and concrete as can be: a smack in the mouth, a cut lip, the taste of blood on the tongue. We know that pain, discomfort of running the edge of the tongue over a sore inside the lip, the salt taste of blood, and we are with her at once. But that story turns out to be the first chapter of a novel in which the world she will lead us into will become more and more strange, surreal, a world which is deep within the imagination the deeper we follow. But we *do* follow because she has made us taste the blood of her world, "proving" its existence to us, coaxing us in by realistic details in a somewhat similar way that fairy tales do. As Bruno Bettelheim points out in his book *The Uses of Enchantment: On the Interpretation of Fairy Tales*, fairy tales "usually start out in a quite realistic way: a mother telling her daughter to go all by herself to visit grandmother..." as the beginning of a series of increasingly mythical, symbolic, and often terrifying occurrences.

Interesting comparisons and contrasts can be made between the ways in which Swan employs verisimilitude and the ways it is used by Gordon Weaver and by Andre Dubus in their stories. Weaver, in his story collection *A World Quite Round*, employs essentially realistic narrative in a variety of ways that veer across realism's borders into regions of intentional anti-illusionism, where he discusses the illusions he is creating and, ironically, in the process, creates an even stronger illusion — that of the truth speaker who destroys illusions. Or else he constructs a kind of shadow story exploring the nature of the language in which the story is told — as with his novella "The Interpreter." Or he deals subtly with the creation of art in general and its relation to identity and existence as in his story "Ah Art! Oh Life!"

In virtually all of Andre Dubus's stories, he has sought his metaphors and meanings in the daily experiences of the lives of his characters in a realism which aims as nearly as possible to imitate a reality experienced by real people in a real world.

But what all these examples have in common is that by manipulating the details of physical or sensory "reality" of the fictional world, the writer creates a dimension to house its psychological and spiritual reality as well: Coover's linguistic island where death is the beginning and blood writes sentences on the wall, Swan's carnival, Weaver's world of language, Camoin's paradox, but also the psychological or spiritual reality of a world like our own, as in the work of Dubus, Carver, and all the other "realists" of our time.

The use of so-called particulars in fiction — objects, sensory impressions — serves more than one purpose; at one and the same time, it enables the writer to create a realistic and a magical world. Alice McDermott says, "We use detail in fiction to tame time, to step on life's receding tail. We use precise detail...not merely because it makes for better, more vivid writing; we use detail because the moment of conscious contact holds a drop of solace."

Thus, the physical detail at once stops time, comforts the reader, and bolsters the realistic illusion. But it does more, it infuses that illusion of reality with magic: "The moment an object appears in a narrative," says Italo Calvino, "it is charged with a special force and becomes like the pole of a magnetic field, a knot in the network of invisible relationships. The symbolism of an object may be more or less explicit, but it is always there. We might even say that in a narrative any object is always magic."

A friend of mine came home from work one day to find his Colombian mother-in-law sitting at his dining table trying to glue together the pieces of one of his favorite vases.

"What happened to it?" he asked. She looked up at him and explained, "A bat flew in the window and knocked it over." His mother-in-law was neither crazy nor stupid, but she had a rich Colombian imagination — her only mistake was in not realizing the sad depths of skepticism and shallowness of imagination of her North American neighbors. In Colombia, I imagine, this explanation of the broken vase would evoke a glimmering aura of magical connections, meanings, interpretations; in New York, it called forth nothing but an unvoiced if amused accusation: "What bullshit."

Psychological and spiritual verisimilitude will also be achieved via the recording of a fictional character's private perceptions — as when Alta, smacked in the mouth by her husband, experiences a sense of danger having entered the roots of her existence.

Such use of verisimilitude to suspend disbelief of a world existing in whole or part beyond the world of the senses, per se, created in a dimension only of sensual *image* or imitation, also calls to mind Hawthorne's definition of fiction as "a neutral territory somewhere between the real world and fairyland where the actual and imaginary may meet and each imbue itself with the nature of the other" and Melville's reference to it as exhibiting "more reality than real life itself can show." Saul Bellow, in *Humboldt's Gift*, performs an amusing and effective reversal, rendering a woman character "real" with a reference to art, by saying she had teeth "like the screaming horse in Picasso's *Guernica*."

Earlier I mentioned John Gardner's view of the concept of verisimilitude — his conception that a fiction of verisimilitude was a wholly realistic one meant to be experienced as occurring in the imagined reflection, if you will, of the world in which we find ourselves — recalling Aristotle's mimetic theory of art. Even Chekhov challenges this when the black monk, in his remarkable story of that title, says, "I exist in your imagination, and your imagination is part of nature which means that I exist in nature, too."

In contrast to Gardner's theory, we have theories such as Jerome Klinkowitz's in *The Practice of Fiction in America*, which refers to the mimetic theory of art as "voodoo," an attempt to substitute the ficiton for what is real.

Alain Robbe-Grillet has said, "...academic criticism in the West as in the communist countries, employs the word 'realism' as if reality were already entirely constituted... when the writer comes on the scene. Thus it supposes that the latter's role is limited to 'explaining' and 'expressing' the reality of his period." This, in opposition to the view of fiction as *creative of reality* — Brecht's hammer, Kafka's axe to chop away the ice of our frozen consciousness.

So now we are back to the question of whether not only "realism" but reality itself is a fiction forged of the language in which it is expressed.

It is interesting to think of this in relation to some examples of political propaganda. Following the troubles in the People's Republic of China in 1989, the Chinese Government began issuing a series of booklets whose aim clearly was to write the history of the events in Tiananmen Square. As they put it in one of their press releases, "At present...many people are not clear about the truth. Therefore, there is a need to explain the truth about the counter-revolutionary rebellion..."

There is a wild beauty in the raging naivete of this which makes me think of some of the tarter fictions of Donald Barthelme where one is hypnotized by statements of blatant paradox: "She comes to him fresh from the bath, opens her robe. 'Goodbye,' she explains, 'Goodbye.'"

One of my favorite of the Chinese propoganda booklets is the one titled "How Chinese View the Riot in Beijing," in which the anonymous propaganda writer composes a number of fictional personas and has them present their "view" of what happened. For example, there is one titled "An Old Worker on the Riot" which begins,

> "I am an ordinary old worker. In the recent period when I saw our sacred and solemn Tiananmen Square become a scene of great disorder and confusion, a filthy place that gave off a strong smell, I felt as if a fire were burning in my heart. In those days, a gang of counter-revolutionary thugs made unbridled attacks on the Chinese Communist Party..."

Clearly a case of political coopting of the fictional technique of realism, verisimilitude, and persona to present a fabricated version of reality, an illusion.

An even more bizarre example can be found in *The Medical Profession and Human Rights Handbook* (New York and London: Zed Books with British Medical Association, 2001) in its exposé of arguments used to support capital punishment by lethal injection via the following summary of a Chinese newspaper report from February 1999:

> "Four individuals had been sentenced to execution on 4 November 1997 and (when they) were told the day before that lethal injection would be used... 'they rejoiced greatly.' During the execution a doctor reportedly asked one of the condemned how it felt. He responded that 'it's good, it doesn't hurt.' It took between 32 and 58 seconds for the men to die."

Of course, the West too uses fictional technique in its propaganda. Amongst my collection, I have a nice sleek booklet entitled, *Ladies and Gentlemen: The 41st President of the United States*, distributed by the United States Information Service immediately after George Bush (the father) was elected and which also seems aimed at the creation of a fictional persona:

> *"George took after his ebullient and empathetic mother. He liked pleasing people. 'He was the easiest child to bring up,' his mother says, 'very obedient.' The Bushes competed at everything — golf, tennis, tiddlywinks — anything that measured one person against another... The concept of family was so powerful that it sometimes seemed to friends that the Bush children functioned as a single mind rather than as five kids fighting for parental affection."*

That single mind concept is kind of scarey — like science fiction, and the concept that a tiddlywinks match measures one person against another... One thinks of Hemingway's imagined fistfights with great European authors of the past.

It works the other way, too. *The Starr Report* investigation into the "Nature of President William Jefferson Clinton's Relationship with Monica Lewinski" reads very much like anti-realism, rather like a postmodern fiction by Harold Jaffe or Robley Wilson, Jr., or Donald Barthelme in which intimate detail is narrated in such rigid prose that it begins to seem surreal or even irreal.

In his fascinating book *Fiction and the Figures of Life*, William H. Gass comments on the mimetic theory of fiction by pronouncing pathetic the view of fiction as creative of living persons rather than of mere characters by pointing out that fiction is made out of words and words only. "It is shocking really," he says, to realize this — rather like discovering after all those years "that your wife is made of rubber."

In *The Art of Fiction*, John Gardner says, "In any piece of fiction, the writer's first job is to convince the reader that the events he recounts really happened...or might have happened (given small changes in the laws of the universe)...The realistic writer's way of making events convincing is verisimilitude." Gardner says that the tools of verisimilitude are "actual settings (Cleveland, San Francisco, Joplin, Missouri), precision of detail... streets, stores, weather, politics, etc., and plausible behavior."

As an example, Gardner names the question, "Would a mother really say that?" — a question he claimed to pose every time a mother in fiction speaks. However, if we look at a piece called "The Philosophers" by Russel Edson, we read this opening:

> *"I think, therefore I am, said a man whose mother quickly hit him on the head saying, I hit my son on his head, therefore I am..."*

According to Gardner's formula, we are obliged to ask ourselves, "Would a mother really say that?"

Well, I don't know, yes and no, she might not *say* it, she might just thump him on the head, actually or metaphorically, without explaining the importance of doing so for her own existential identity. Perhaps it presents a deeper level of reality of her behavior, of the relationship between son and mother, of human modes of existential identification. In other words, a mother might or might not actually say and do such a thing, but one recognizes immediately that this is not the point, that a reality is being presented via details that *could* occur, even if they are absurd, and thus here exists verisimilitude: we have a son, a mother, action, speech. A son speaks, is hit, answered. It *could* have happened. We laugh or curl our toes. It is absurd, but it is also true, reveals a hidden reality in a very efficient manner, and really it doesn't matter at all whether it ever happened or is meant to have happened: we have followed Edson into a dimension of the imagination as surely as when we follow Alice through the looking glass.

Russel Edson is good at this sort of thing:

Father throws the baby in the air. The baby hits the ceiling. Stop, says mother, the ceiling is crying, you're hurting the ceiling.

Would a mother really say that? Well, it is not inconceivable that some mother at some time whose little boy runs headlong into her Louis Quartorze writing table and falls bleeding profusely from the scalp upon her 19th century Persian carpet may have been heard to scream "Oh God" My poor table! My beautiful carpet! You clumsy fool!" That, too, is a kind of verisimilitude in certain cases.

"A bat flew in the window and knocked it over." Would a mother-in-law really say that? I have only my friend's word for it, but I believe it; even if it is a lie, I believe it.

Of course, it all comes down to the question, What is real? To many people, life sometimes seems little more than a series of repetitions of meaningless events: we rise, we eat, we go to work, we come home again, we eat, look at the tube, sleep, rise again, etc. If that is what our lives really have become, a story like Robert Coover's "The Elevator" — written in rebellion against standard realism and the conventional view of an orderly reality, and depicting a series of scenes of a man entering his office building each day to ride up to his office and the adventures he experiences during those few minutes, each scene a kind of parody of a literary style — is perhaps more realistic than surrealistic, even though the events depicted are far from conventional ones and the intention is perhaps more theoretical than representational.

Perhaps such a fiction employs verisimilitude to portray an "unreal" world that reflects something more essential of contemporary existence than a story built on linear plot and movement in which a meaningful progression of events is depicted, leading from beginning through complication of logical occurrences and cause and effect to a climax and resolution.

Jimmy Carter, nearly thirty years ago, looked directly into a television camera and, imagining the American public before him, said, "I want you to listen carefully now. I will never tell you a lie."

Applying John Gardner's verisimilitude test to that, we may ask ourselves, Would an American President really say that? But he did, just as William Jefferson Clinton, two decades later, would look into a nationwide camera and pronounce, "I did *not* have sexual relations with that woman." Where Carter's statement was perhaps a mere well-meant but naive and self-deluding pronouncement, Clinton's would later show itself to be a postmodernistic manipulation of language of breathtaking skill. The illusion is always in the language. Add two or three words to Al Gore's statement about inventing the internet — say, "early fostered the *idea* of" — and the result is interest instead of scorn; just as when young Dubya Bush refers to Greeks as "Grecians," with one word he creates the unshakeable image of a man abysmally ill-informed in international affairs.

Unlike Jimmy Carter and like Bill Clinton, a fiction writer must select, manipulate, eliminate, foreshorten, lie — and he must do it in the interests of a truth greater than what can be found in our confusing everyday reality. A writer may lie by seeming to duplicate reality or by seeming to destroy it — the anti-illusionist we see at work for example in John Barth's *The Floating Opera* and *Lost in the Funhouse*. Barth begins *The Floating Opera* by having his first person creative narrator tell the reader that he has never written a novel before but has read a few to try to get the hang of it — immediately convincing the reader, duping him, into believing that this is not fiction, but a straight-from-the-heart account. Anti-illusion becomes in this way an even stronger illusion.

Most readers probably don't give much thought to the fact that the prounoun "I" in a fiction almost always is every bit the fictional persona as the pronoun "he" or "she," a created character, a mask the author holds before his or her face as the actors did in Greek tragedies. This is a concept Robert Pinsky professes to be liberated of: "When I say I (in a poem), I mean whatever it is that I mean when I say I in speaking to you. The poem is something that Robert says — that is not to say that Robert is, in my mind, a stable entity...in a sense, persona and archetype are not any more conditions of literature than they are of life for me...the idea of persona...was in style when I was in college; one of the great liberating and enabling moments for me was when i was able to decide I wasn't going to pay attention to it."

This is an interesting approach; however, for most fiction writers, I am convinced it applies to no extent greater than that which applied to Flaubert when he said, *"Madame Bovary, c'est moi."*

And one can scarcely avoid the fact that, for example, writing a story with a first person child narrator necessarily limits the author's use of language and observational sophistication while the same story in third person could bear the expression of a more mature consciousness to relate the child's story, with the child's sensibility cast into a richer, more mature language. The same effect, of course, can be achieved in first person with a time distance, a moment of narration cast well into the future, but this only further illustrates the fact that the personal pronoun *I* is rarely a simple matter.

"I, *I*! ...the filthiest of all the pronouns," said Carlo Emilio Gadda. "They are the lice of thought. When a thought has lice, it scratches, like everyone with lice...and in your fingernails, then...you find pronouns: the personal pronouns."

On the matter of dogmatic realism in fiction, when Ezra Pound complained to James Joyce that *Finnegans Wake* was obscure, Joyce answered, "Well now, Ezra, the action of my work takes place at night. It is natural, isn't it, that things should not be so clear at night?"

We have probably all seen spy films in which the action at night is so realistically depicted that we are left completely in the dark as to what is happening. The point is, we don't have to *use* darkness to fictionalize the dark. We use words, impressions, and our aim in fiction is to elucidate the deeper reality of darkness, not to reproduce a sensation of being in the dark for the sake of that sensation alone.

I believe that an examination of virtually every fictional mode will show that verisimilitude is an element at work in all of them, that in a large sense all fiction writers are "realists," in that all are dealing with reality.

Realism is only one of a number of available artistic illusions, all of which depend for their plausibility on some measure of verisimilitude.

In Gladys Swan's novel *Carnival for the Gods*, a carnival illusionist, a sleight-of-hand "artist" who, in popular terms, is known as a "magician," is approached by a boy who believes the man's magic to be real and who asks to be taught the secrets of that art. The man is so unnerved by the boy's faith in magic that he lies to him and pretends that he *can* teach magic to the child in hopes that he will divert the boy from falling into evil secrets.

But the boy is undaunted. When, finally, the illusionist dies, the boy still believes that he can find what he seeks. He takes the dead magician's cape and goes off on his own, determined to search for what he seeks and, in the closing words of the book, "if he didn't find it, to create it in an imagined land."

I find this a concise and powerful summary of the process of art. Wrapped in the mantle of a fake circus magician, the artist sets out to imagine a land in which truth can be created.

For the fiction writer, verisimilitude is the tool of the imaginative act by which that truth is sought, the soil in which an imaginary garden can grow and provide a home for the toads of that which is genuine.

And it is the same for the realist and for the innovator, the experimenter, the task is the same. All is permitted.

 JOSHUA MCKINNEY

Couch

I wish I had never fallen asleep on the couch. Defenseless there, with a beer and a book, I was consumed. Sometime later I awoke on my back inside it, cramped, arms crossed over my chest and unable to move. I've shouted myself mute, but the stuffing muffles my cries. Occasionally some crumbs sift down through the cushions. Maybe a peanut, a kernel of popcorn. Two coins tumbled down and landed over my eyes. The worst part is when people use it—the pressure on my chest, the lack of air. Like last night when the detective dropped by again and he and my wife whispered into the wee hours. Or this morning when the kids jumped up and down on my balls playing trampoline, no one to stop them now.

A Sentence Is a Snake

I'm reading in bed when I find my mind has wandered. I reread a stanza and it still seems unfamiliar. I put the book on the bedside table and turn off the lamp. Cross my hands on my chest. Close my eyes. In that half state—not waking, not sleep—I see an old woman in overalls and a ball cap. Smoking a hand-rolled cigarette. She's seventy-seven and says some day she is going to write the story of her life. It has been an interesting life, she says, full of hardship and triumph. A fit of coughing shakes her and she struggles to catch her breath. Then she leans toward me. Look here, she says: "A sentence is a snake." If she says anything else, I don't hear. I'm too focused on the line, which is how I have already begun to think of it. A sentence is a snake. It's a good line—great, in fact. So great that when I write it down I'm sure a poem will bloom without effort around it and the lines of that poem will turn of their own accord—sinuous, mysterious, beautiful. It will be my best poem. The one I have waited for these many years. But I am so tired, already slipping into sleep. I repeat the line over and over: a sentence is a snake a sentence is a snake a sentence is a snake a sentence

The Death of the Author

When I was a boy I played between my father's legs. No. I am disturbed that you would think that. When Mom was at work he would sit in the big, overstuffed chair and read from his big book. His feet up on the foot stool. I would crawl beneath his outstretched legs and press my head up between them. No. Your insinuations disgust me. It was nothing like that. He would bend his knees slightly outward and the hatch to my U-boat would open. I would raise my head up between his Levied thighs. Scan the sea's edge for convoys. If all was clear I would take the fresh air awhile. Sometimes a destroyer might surprise us and he would give the order to dive and I would go down and the hatch would close over me. Run silent. Run deep. No. Must you see sickness in everything? You and your metaphors, your double entendres. Have you no shame? You have stolen my childhood.

David Eric Tomlinson
THE ORNITHOLOGIST'S LAST WISH

The geese are winging in from the north. First a hairline thread in the muted horizon, then a cross-stitch in the sky over Portaferry, in County Down, Northern Ireland. Soon a dark and honking seam gliding in against the ebbing tidal narrows, breaking rank at last to alight in ungainly spray atop the waters of Strangford Lough, an inlet sheltered from the Irish sea by the crooked finger of the Ards Peninsula.

A couple walks along the rocky mudflats edging the shoreline, waiting for the birds. The man moves with purpose, always several steps ahead of his wife, skipping across minor tide pools with a grace belying his age. She is easily distracted, and the man often finds himself waiting, neck craned past his shoulder, as the woman bends to examine some newly discovered piece of the landscape. Garbage fascinates her: cigarette butts, discarded beer bottles, bits of plastic packaging tumbling in the surf. A half-buried Styrofoam cup can elicit soft murmurs of wonder.

The woman is an ornithologist, and calls herself Newt. Newt cups caramel fingers around thin lips and a sequence of modulated honks trumpets from her throat, the practiced performance pitching across seething whitecaps. The birds are intrigued. A white-faced gander rises from the water to investigate, dark neck pumping under a gray, feathered flurry. Newt's braying intensifies, and for a moment it appears woman and bird might embrace, an absurd marriage of heaven and earth, until the approaching goose banks widely away, complaining loudly at the ruse. The bird glides a graceful arc back to the gaggle, silver tail feathers flashing in the gray morning light.

Newt has lured her husband here to overwinter with a flock of barnacle geese she's studying, something about the dialect of bird calls in rural areas as compared to urban centers. They've rented the top floor of a bed and breakfast in Strangford proper. The village is much changed since their last visit together, in the early seventeenth century, when Newt was working as scribe to an Anglican churchman intent on translating *The Book of Common Prayer* into the Goidelic languages. Back then, they sailed for Dublin in a passenger galley stinking of stale bilge water. Newt remembers wooden bouts with boredom, a stiffness settling into her calves, hurly-burly debarkations into lurching, beast-drawn vehicles.

This year the trip was more pleasant; they flew *Aer Lingus* to Dublin, rented a car, and arrived in less than a day.

The man goes by Gage, and he is over seven thousand years old, only a handful of years older than Newt. He's drawn to more exotic destinations, cities where every leaf and pavestone still resonates with the great and terrible vanity of man: Cairo, Saint Petersburg, Hiroshima, Los Angeles. But Newt has hinted that Strangford holds a surprise, knowing full well that after seven millennia of watching history chase its tail, her husband places a premium on the unknown.

It's been almost a century since their last reunion, in Rome. They were picnicking near the worn cobblestones of the Appian Way, remembering the stately spectacle of the Roman army marching south to war, when Nuit (for this is her real name) announced that, heretofore, she would only answer to the name *Newt*.

"Newt?" Gage asked. "Like the salamander?"

In answer to her husband's question, Newt had covered her lips with a hand, leaned back, and laughed into the high, bright air.

Perched upon a mossy boulder, Gage watches Newt try to lure the birds nearer to shore, her voice mimicking the cacophony coming from the water. Her beauty has compounded through the years; what was once a shiny trinket is now a hypnotic, lustrous intricacy that leaves him puzzled. There is something almost cinematic in her gestures. A kind of nostalgic undertow, always pulling him back. They have walked together upon too many beaches to count, seen flocks of birds teeming so thickly up from the earth that the sun looked veiled. But today they are walking on *this* beach, and Newt is singing to *this* flock of birds. And it reminds Gage of how simple life was before they met the magician.

They were both born hopelessly mortal, surfacing from oblivion in the waning days of the Neolithic, five thousand years prior to what the Gregorian calendar would one day label the birth of Christ. They found themselves indentured into servitude under an autocratic tribal chieftain named Geb, member of a quarrelsome bloodline which eventually tapered off with the rise of the Scorpion King, the pharaoh Serqet, almost two thousand years later.

Gage pecked out a hardscrabble subsistence working the lush deltas of the Nile river valley, harvesting wheat and tubers from the warm, dark earth. The long days shaped him into a lean instrument. He was a tireless and good-natured farmer, eagerly absorbing centuries-old secrets about sowing and irrigation from the village elders, then passing the knowledge along to his three younger brothers.

He knew Newt only as a playmate of his youngest brother. A bright-eyed girl from a hard-working family, Newt was cheerful and talkative—nothing more than an annoyance, in the beginning. But one afternoon, after a rainy season so severe the engorged Nile had leapt its banks to lap at the fringes of their village, Gage heard Newt singing. He was instantly enraptured. Gage can still hear her sweet voice lilting above the flooded farmland, entertaining her father as the man rowed his plot of land repairing damaged dykes. Newt was no more than a girl of thirteen seasons, but Gage was patient. He volunteered to help her father with the harvest, learned to laugh at her jokes, and waited.

At the time, it seemed to Gage that his courtship of Newt would last an eternity, though in reality it took a mere four seasons for Gage to convince Newt's father that he was a suitable match for his daughter. In those days, a man was fortunate to live beyond three dozen seasons, and the bloody rigors of childbirth made widowers of many. Gage submitted to interminable, supervised visits with his future bride, the two of them talking quietly together as a hawkish brood of aunts, cousins, and sisters hovered nearby. Eventually, they were married in midnight ritual, beneath a sky not yet dulled by electric light.

Gage was appointed the tribe's structural engineer by the chieftain, charged with maintaining the levees that siphoned water from the ceaseless flow of the Nile. He stumbled home each night and clung to Newt in their hut of mud and straw. As the seasons wore on, the rains delivered a few months of welcome respite from his toil, but the incessant floods eroded Gage's handiwork. Each spring he was forced to begin again, as if all the days past had never occurred. He became inured to transience, accustomed to a constant state of frailty.

Gage first found the magician trying to liberate one of his two prized goats, the man's soiled and pilferous fingernails working at the latch gate to the livestock enclosure. A wall-eyed and wrinkled gypsy from the northern tribes, the creature's dark, mottled skin stank of wild onions and musk. Gage's impulse was to cleave the thief through the riblets with his scythe, but Newt begged him to spare the creature. She invited him into their meager house for supper, where the beggar sat splayed upon their reed mat floor, slurping soup from grimy fingers.

"Why do you not kill me?" The vagabond asked. "Surely the earth will not miss one less thieving old man."

"My wife is more generous than I am," Gage said. "And it's my duty to give her what she wants."

The man's good eye twinkled at Gage's reply, the other fixing Newt with a cloudy retina blooming with cataracts. He prompted her for another petition: "Wish again! Test the limits of your husband's resolve! What do you desire, above all things?"

Newt considered the game impolite, and did not rise to the man's baiting. Thinking him harmless, she allowed the beggar to bed down with the animals. Gage thought differently, and hogtied him in the hay until morning. They awoke to find Gage's cinch knots lying empty in the straw, both of the goats now gone missing. It had taken more than a year to save enough for the goat kids, another year to raise them to mating age. They would need to start afresh, toiling in the tribal fields for another season at least, until the livestock could be replaced.

"Ashes!" Newt shouted, disturbing a crow perched atop the fence post. "How could I have been so foolish? I'll answer the filthy prowler now. Do you know what I really want? To be wealthy beyond my dreams. I want to bathe in goat milk."

The crow shook dew from tattered plumage and leapt aloft, wings flapping.

Newt spat into the sand, her good will run dry, and the first wish was sealed.

It happened like this:

Three nights after the beggar stole away with their animals, Gage found himself in the tribal wheat field near dusk, helping with the harvest. Eager tongues of lightning licked at the far hills. Fearing he would lose his way in the approaching storm, Gage decided to take a short cut for home, through the neighboring gardens of the sun cult. If discovered, he would be punished by the priests. But their god abhorred the darkness ... they were likely already ensconced in their temple, transported by evening chants.

Gage jogged through the wheat, leapt the far bank of an irrigation ditch, and padded into a copse of baobab and palm trees. He crept through the well-tended terraces, charmed by a potent perfume of jasmine and honeysuckle. The sounds of his passage were muted by plaintive calls from the night herons and ibis nestled in the fronds overhead. He could see the torchlit walls of the temple flickering in the middle distance. A faint drumbeat emanated from the building, the steady pulse of priestly nightsong reverberating against the curdling dark. As Gage neared the far reaches of the garden he heard the cadence of hushed voices.

"... arrives with his guards tomorrow. But he has agreed to a private council. With me."

"Alone? You're sure?" Gage heard the distinct timbre of the high priest's voice.

"A small contingent of guards. But my men can overpower them."

"Tomorrow evening, then."

"The payment?"

"Half now, half once it's done," the priest said.

"Yes."

"The chieftain will pay even more dearly. His death will not be mourned here."

"How will you explain the death of your village leader?"

"That won't be necessary," said the high priest. "I will lead them."

"Will they follow?"

"With you and your men at my side? They will have to."

Gage knelt low and tried to slow his breathing. Squinting in the direction of the voices, he blinked back a diffuse afterglow vexing his vision. The shapes of two men soon resolved behind a thick cane break—the high priest of the sun cult whispering to a swarthy stranger clad in dark robes. The men spoke again, shoulders hunched close, then separated. The slap of their sandals receded into opposite halves of the night.

Gage's insides threatened to spill out onto the ground. He guessed that the stranger was an assassin from the northern tribes, likely hired from the same stock as the thief who'd just stolen his goats. His heart held no special sanctuary for the chieftain, whose impulses could be inconvenient at times. But he was a fair ruler, and abused his power only rarely. Newt was only a sometimes worshipper at the temple of the sun god, and had always considered their brand of piety a mostly self-serving enterprise.

He hurried home to find Newt waiting up for him, a dinner of rice and tubers cooling on the floor. Gage recounted the night's adventure, watching the creases in Newt's forehead deepen as he spoke. His story finished, they sat together in a bloated silence.

Gage feared retribution from the high priest and his followers, should he interfere with the cult's plans. Newt feared the guilt that inaction might deliver; she could not imagine their future tainted by the chieftain's blood. Neither of them wanted to make a decision.

Newt began murmuring to herself, toying with the available courses of action. She was still so young, and clung to a belief that words could act as a kind of moral compass. As if discussion might reveal a truth which would otherwise remain obscured. They debated through that night, a meandering disquisition on self-preservation and responsibility, which concluded with Gage setting out for the chieftain's estate at first light, to warn him of the impending attempt on his life.

Gage approached the tribal stronghold, explaining to a stern cadre of sentinels that he carried a private message for their leader Geb. Flanked by two mute bodyguards armed with flashing, leaden scythes, Gage was escorted into the chieftain private quarters, where he described what he'd overheard. As he spoke, an erratic bloodrush pounded in Gage's temples. For a moment everything seemed to vibrate, and he heard what sounded like the faint trilling of birds. He rushed to complete his tale, voice faltering, unsure what to make of this nervous onslaught. When he was done Gage glanced over at his escorts. Both men were silent, oblivious to the barely discernible birdsong which was—even now—fading into obscurity.

Geb seemed to listen quite carefully to Gage's story, but then dismissed him with the wave of a hand. Worrying what would come from his tale of the planned assassination, uncertain what the chieftain might be thinking, Gage returned to the fields, where he continued to labor each day. Each night he returned along the well-worn footpath to home, and to Newt.

A week passed, then two. One morning Gage surfaced from acrid dreams of hot, burning fields, having almost forgotten the episode. He awoke to the smell of *real* ashes, thin shadows wisping past the open doorframe. Gage and Newt rushed outside to find thick pillars of smoke snaking up into a cloudless sky. They heard the sharp crack of a whip and saw a shackled line of men shuffling from the smoldering temple nearby: the bedraggled members of the sun cult. The chieftain's guards shouted coarse commands at their new prisoners.

That afternoon, Gage was summoned to the chieftain's estate. In exchange for a promise to supply the tribe with a portion of his yearly harvest, Gage was granted two dozen slaves, a bodyguard, and a small herd of goats, which he marched triumphantly into the house that very evening. As Newt scrambled to salvage their dinner from the greedy mouths of their new herd, Gage felt the beginnings of a laugh bubble up from somewhere deep inside his belly.

"Your wish has come true!" He said. "Should I draw the milk for your bath now ... or would you prefer to wait until morning?"

***

They enjoyed a honeymoon of sorts, a near decade of leisure. Gage remembers blissful summer days with Newt, their extended bouts of lovemaking interrupted only by the occasional meal. And what meals they were! Enormous loaves of bread, which Newt would tear into fist-sized servings to be dipped in olive oil; sun-dried fishes garnished with wild onions; spiced meats and juicy figs; and a thick barley wine which had the tendency to inspire thoughts of more lovemaking.

Newt bore three sons, and they were happy, all of them together, for a time.

But the former followers of the sun cult, who now toiled as slave labor in the tribal fields, nursed an infective rancor for the chieftain. As Gage and Newt enjoyed their newfound prosperity, watching their sons grow tall among the gardens they now tended, subversive seeds were being sown among the thick rows of wheat and barley. The chieftain's response to the threat on his life had been swift and severe: the high priest and his inner circle were branded as traitors and executed in a bloody public ceremony, the severed stumps of their heads mounted atop sharp stakes as warning sign to others. There were few records of such violence in the tribe's oral histories, and unbeknownst to Gage a rebellion began to take root in the village, a popular discontent which soon twisted the minds of his neighbors into a tangle of suspicion and resentment.

Almost ten seasons to the day that Gage walked triumphantly into his hut with a new herd of goats, a horde of villagers overthrew the chieftain and his guards. Armed with knives and torches, the angry mob then descended upon Gage's estate. He awoke to the eager crackle and pop of wooden beams burning. Behind the panicked bleats coming from the livestock enclosure, he heard the rise and fall of shouted voices. He shook Newt awake. Without speaking they gathered up their sons and ran barefoot into the darkened fields, eventually stopping to huddle together against the inhospitable chill cast by a new moon, which stared blankly down at them from the star-speckled sky.

As his family tried to sleep through that first night, a clammy panic descended upon Gage. They had been cast from their village like lepers, forced to fend for themselves beyond the dim fringes of the watch fires, where the anguished calls of the spirit beasts could be heard roaming in the nearby bush. Neither Gage nor Newt guessed that the beggar's magic was at work. They did not yet understand that this was just the first of many flights: past the fixed boundaries of prosperity and into the shifting, borderless wasteland of the needy, where survival would depend, more often than not, on a quick wit and the good humor of strangers.

Nor could they have known, when their youngest son fell ill with fever and died, two weeks into their journey downriver, that the yawning, bottomless hurt which soon swallowed their hearts would be repeated, over and again, for as long as they lived.

Now it's Christmas, in 2009. They sit sipping tea in a Portaferry café, across the water from Strangford, talking about the birds.

"Did you know they're monogamous?" Newt says.

"I did know that."

"Did you know the word *barnacle* originated with these birds? The villagers thought the hatchlings issued, fully-formed, from the shell-encrusted knots under the driftwood, as it bobbed through the narrows during high tide. This was, oh five hundred years ago, give or take. Before they understood migration patterns." She lapses into a rarefied dialect of Gaelic. "*The townsfolk would crawl out of their beds in early winter to find a gaggle of geese frolicking on the strand. Not an egg in sight.*"

"Before, there were no birds," Gage says. "Then there were birds."

"Ergo ... magic."

"Say *ergo* again."

"*Stop it.*" Again in Gaelic.

"I've missed you," Gage says. "Let's go back to the hotel and I'll prove it."

"*What have we been doing for the past four days? There will be plenty of time for that later. I have to tell you the best part.*"

"What's the best part?"

"*I'll tell you.*" She switches back to English. "Because there were no eggs. Because the birds just showed up every winter, like magic. Because they simply ... *coalesced.*"

"Finish the story."

"Because of the strange origins of these ... *magic geese* ... the locals didn't consider them birds. Their flesh wasn't classified as fowl. So during Lent ..."

"Aha! Now I see. These country folk can be quite shrewd when they're hungry."

"*They could eat the birds without fear of perdition,*" Newt says in Gaelic.

"So if the geese weren't birds ... then what were they?"

"*Something new,*" she replies. "*Something never before seen under the sun.*"

"Something old, something new," Gage says.

A young couple enters the café, the hollow chime from a bell affixed to the door jamb announcing their arrival. An infant is strapped across the woman's chest, sleeping soundly in a bright blue sort of satchel, chubby arms and legs splayed every which way as her head rests cradled between her mother's breasts.

Newt falls silent, eyes misting over at the sight of the child. She twirls a brown plastic coffee stirrer deftly between her fingers, staring out the window at the silvery expanse of the narrows. On the far side of the Lough the hills of Strangford float above a shifting foundation of fog.

Gage has often tried to delineate the boundary between where their marriage ends and the magician's curse begins. But things are no longer so simple. The dark calculus of immortality has been working at his memories, adding clarity and texture to seemingly insignificant moments, reducing truly momentous events to mere fragments.

He can remember his first plane flight in exquisite detail: the hum of the propellers outside, the pattern of the fabric on the seats. And the smells: coffee and poached eggs, the tart tang of cigarette smoke, the overpowering perfume wafting from the pale curve of the flight attendant's neck. Gage drew that thick potpourri into his lungs and—for the first time in his eternal, deathless life—looked down upon the clouds from heights he'd thought were possible only in dreams.

And yet he can recall only the vaguest impressions of the years following their son's death. They spent their days in exile, living in a distant village which straddled the Nile. Gage fed his family by cultivating and distilling barley into an amber-colored wine that soon became one of the most prized possessions in town. He managed to strike up a few fast friendships with his neighbors, but Newt withdrew, sinking into a dark despondency. She spent the better part of her days hiding in the shuttered shelter of their home, fretting over their two remaining boys, each of whom eventually retreated from her attentions, decamping separately into the hoggish myopia of puberty.

One spring, now early in the fifth millennium Before Christ, and only a few decades after they had fled their home, Gage found the beggar scrounging around their newly built wine cellar; or perhaps the man simply materialized, unannounced, at the door, begging for a jug of wine and a night's refuge from the rains. In any case, Gage was furious, and demanded to know the fate of his stolen goats. But Newt seemed to soften in the old man's company. Relieved to see a familiar face, she invited him in for another dinner. As the three of them emptied first one and then a second skin of wine, the magician waved bony fingers about the room and began quizzing Newt.

"Your first wish," the old man asked, "it came true?"

"What do you mean?" Newt asked.

"You were rich beyond your wildest imaginings, yes?"

"We were," Newt said. "But never for long."

"You seem to be prospering here," said the magician.

Newt said "Our son died when we fled the village."

Sitting cross-legged on the floor, Gage realized that he was drunk. He leaned backwards, closing his eyes, and braced himself against the wall. The room seemed to move with him, spinning end-over-end into his eyelids.

He heard the magician splutter, then admit to casting some kind of spell— "Just a trifle!" the old man explained to Newt—and that as thanks for their previous hospitality, wealth would come easily to them now ... though it might dissipate suddenly, and without warning. When Newt pressed him for details the magician hedged. He was still perfecting his craft! There was still much for him to learn!

Gage opened his eyes. Newt had risen from her seat upon the floor, and now paced slow circles between Gage and their visitor, working herself up into a cheerless dudgeon.

"A pox on your crooked magic!" Newt finally said. "It's because of *you* that we were banished from our home! Because of *you* that our son fell ill during the escape!"

"I am truly sorry," the magician said.

"Had we never met you," Newt said, "we could have all lived there happily. Forever."

The magician blinked. "Nothing lasts forever," he said.

Newt leapt howling across the table. Dishes and cutlery clattered to the floor as she tried to claw at the man's throat. Gage pulled his wife away from the old man, cutting his hand on a jagged stone knife in the process. He shouted at the magician to leave. Newt slumped sobbing into Gage's shirt as their guest scuttled sideways out of the house.

"I just want us to be happy. What is it that they say in fables? I want us to live happily ever after. I want it more with every breath I draw," Newt said. "Don't you?"

Gage heard the distant cry of a crane rise above the stillness beyond his window. He licked at the crimson trail of blood traversing his palm, then kissed his wife squarely on the lips.

"I do," he said.

The magician plied a rough sort of magic, powerful but imperfect, and the couple soon discovered that happily-ever-after comes at a cost.

It was at their oldest son's funeral that Gage finally understood: something was amiss. Their son died of an abscessed tooth at the advanced age of forty-two seasons, a not uncommon path into the afterlife in those days. During the ceremony Gage looked up, blinded by grief, and for a moment mistook Newt for his son's grieving widow. Even at nearly sixty seasons, Newt still looked as vibrant as most of the young mothers in the village. Not a single gray hair defiled her long, dark tresses. And Gage, now the oldest surviving member of the village, still held his own during the summer harvests, bending and threshing in the honeyed fields of wheat alongside his much younger neighbors. His steps were still buoyant with youth; not a single tooth had been lost to either injury or decay.

They were no strangers to despair. Their own children had been fruitful, blessing them with eight surviving grandchildren, and great-grandchildren now arriving with increasing regularity. But four grandchildren had *not* survived, each ravaged by strange fevers in those first, frail months of life. Gage could almost feel himself diminish, bit by bit, as his loved ones passed on into oblivion. And Newt took each loss like a hammer blow to the soul, floundering in ever-darker depths with each fresh death.

"This pain," Newt said. "It's not ... *natural*. We should have joined them a long time ago."

"Soon enough," Gage promised. "One day, our time will come."

But their time never did come. When Gage reached seventy seasons he began to overhear rumors, of a beastly witchcraft he employed to slow the sands of time. At eighty, his neighbors no longer acknowledged him. And at ninety Gage was confronted by the village priest, who warned that if he and Newt did not leave town within the week, they would both be sacrificed as necromancers, their corpses abandoned as fodder for the scavenger vultures sometimes seen circling the skies.

And so it was that one sunny day, nearly seven thousand years ago, Gage and Newt again fled their home, forsaking everything they held dear. Afraid they might attract the further displeasure of the villagers, they left without fanfare, waving casually to their children's children (and their children) as they walked uncremoniously past their homes, just another aged couple enjoying a stroll in early spring: through the center of the village thoroughfare and beyond, where the road narrowed into a footpath, which curved down to wind along the banks of the Nile, until finally being overrun by undergrowth, miles from their home, as it diverged from the river's edge.

The couple stepped off the path, fingers intertwined, and ventured onto the less firm footing of the unremitting future.

***

Gage is driving Newt across the wintry countryside in a cramped rental car smelling of fresh leather and stale air freshener. A new year is approaching—it will be 2010 in a few short days—and Newt has decided it's time to unveil her surprise, hidden somewhere in the wind-worn desert of limestone grikes and brittle, clutching grasses edging Ireland's western shores. The exposed *karren* clefts of the Burren poke through the earth at irregular angles beyond the windshield.

"You're lost," she says. "Just admit it."

"I'm not lost," Gage replies. "What does the map say?"

"It says you're lost."

Gage is feeling hopeful today; they've managed to sustain a mood of genuine affection for several weeks now, languishing in the miracle of the other's presence with a cautious kind of optimism. Newt's research on the geese is nearing a conclusion: freed from worry, she seems strangely sanguine, even in such close proximity to Gage. Normally by now the magician's curse should have started working at their words, twisting what one said or the other heard, until the lines of communication are transposed beyond repair. But not this time. Something is changed, and Gage can only hope that they have finally broken loose from the old man's wizardry.

He remembers the shuddersome realization, a few decades after abandoning their village, that the future would not be bent to their childlike expectations of it. They had alternated between a state of extreme abundance and abject poverty, and these seesawing cycles of fortune and penury had become familiar, even expected. They tested the limits of their newfound immortality, avoiding the perils of sickness, injury, and death at every turn. They could not be killed, and they would never grow old.

But one hundred years of loss had been compounded by the gradual onset of worrisome habits and a lifetime of minor faults, now magnified under the intimidating lens of eternity. The farther they traveled from home and their grandchildren, the darker Newt's moods swings became, and the more Gage found himself only half pretending to listen to his wife's concerns. As they struggled against the hard-hearted inertia of the years it occurred to Gage that they might live happily ever after ... but not together. The magician's flawed magic had taken root, and the only thing each now wanted from the other was solitude.

They first parted on Newt's one hundred and seventeenth birthday, and in the catalog of his many failings over the centuries – poorly-written poems, failed debts, confidences misplaced, lost bets—the wrench of failure felt on that day still reigns supremely in Gage's gut. He wanted more than anything to rise above a history that had somehow turned on them. If he could find some way for them to escape the magician's spell—even momentarily—Gage thought they might achieve some small measure of shared happiness.

Gage traveled east, hoping to discover some antidote to their calamity along the spice routes rumored to extend beyond the limits of the world. Within a few weeks of their initial, experimental estrangement, Gage felt a heady wave of relief rush over him: for the first time in his life, he was totally, utterly free. He began to comprehend the limitless possibilities that an eternity on earth might hold in store.

But the longer they remained apart, the tighter Newt's hold over Gage seemed to become. Somewhere, he knew, she too was free ... free from *him*. Did Newt feel the same existential lift in his absence? Was she liberated, emboldened, transformed? Did she miss him? There were innumerable attempts at reconciliation, of course: long months together (sometimes years) spent trying to recreate those first days, so full of intimacy and abandon, when everything was new. They met in sprawling, dusty cities to make eyes at one another over twelve-course feasts. They made love on the finest Persian rugs, Newt hidden behind flowing veils and a sloe-black eye shadow which made her eyes shine white against the lavender half light. But no matter how earnestly they clung together, the old arguments would begin to pull them apart, almost from the moment they reunited. They threw themselves desperately into self-improvement: Newt, to forget the dogging pain of losing her children; Gage, to remember that his attentiveness was an essential ingredient to Newt's happiness.

None of it helped. They were doomed to oscillate between a state of feverish attraction and highly-charged repulsion, roaming the growing cities of the globe like two lonely poles, sometimes crossing paths in brief and spectacular fashion. Their reunions became a kind of devilish sport, each trying to impress the other with evidence of some newfound capacity for compassion or understanding. Sometimes they would meet two or three times in a decade, hopscotching the continents like newlyweds on safari. Eventually, though, words began to fail them. Soon after, the arguments would begin, and they would quit one another to resume their wandering, reuniting decades or centuries later to retrace the thread of that last discussion. Gage once saw Newt nurture a slow-burning vitriol for over three hundred years, only recovering after he dropped by uninvited with a squirming dachshund puppy, which she promptly named Guy.

Gage learned several dozen languages, navigating the globe as a salesman, entrepreneur, diplomat, trader and wildcatter. He developed an appetite for the close-quartered rubric of commerce, mastering the pressing of palms and the delivery of gentle reassurances as he raised and lost fortunes almost beyond comprehension. Newt took Gage's love of languages several steps further, picking apart songs, poems, sonnets, proclamations—anything she could find that might help her understand the riddle of their predicament. She had a theory that the answer resided in their voices, in the words they relied upon to express love, desire, or indifference. Newt developed a working knowledge of nearly every language ever spoken, hoping to uncover some elemental means of communication that might short-circuit the magician's curse.

Eventually Newt grew disillusioned with her quest, and in the late eighteenth century she abandoned her linguistic studies. Retreating into seclusion once again, she bought a canary—only a hatchling, really—to elevate her sinking spirits. Impatient for the young bird to begin singing, Newt would whistle snippets of Mozart and Haydn to the thing each morning, coaching the bird along. To Newt's great delight and surprise, she awoke one morning to the sound of the canary singing a perfect rendition of Fiordiligi's aria "*Per pietà, ben mio, perdona*" from *Cosi Fan Tutte*. Like a mother teaching her child to speak, Newt had unwittingly taught the bird to sing ... and opera, at that.

Thus began Newt's obsession with ornithology, and the grace that it implied.

"Tell me what you've learned from the birds," Gage says, still driving through western Ireland.

"What?"

"You said they sing differently out here than in the city."

"Yes."

"You seemed very excited about it."

Newt sits quietly in the passenger seat and weighs her reply.

"Turn left," she says.

"Why?"

"We're almost there."

"Where?" Gage asks. He turns onto the barest traces of a worn dirt track, angling away from the main highway to bisect a barren field. The car bounces enthusiastically across a cattle guard, the muffler sometimes sounding a static roar as it drags atop the grassy berm separating the ruts in the road, which crests a squat hill to end in the driveway of a small stone cottage draped with vines.

"This is the surprise?" Gage asks.

"Let's go inside."

Gage stretches his legs as Newt knocks gently at the front door, which creaks slowly open on loose hinges. A throaty voice emerges from the far recesses of the house, instructing them to come in. Gage follows Newt inside, past an orderly entryway, down a mirrored hallway, and on into a wood-paneled media room piled floor to ceiling with books, records, videos and vinyl records. Seated upon a leather recliner in the center of the room, surrounded by stereo equipment and the bluish blink of several television screens, is the magician.

Newt hugs the wizened little man and he smiles, revealing two rows of perfectly white teeth. He looks smaller than Gage remembers, thinner, maybe a few years older ... but definitely more well-groomed, having obviously discovered the miracles of modern dentistry.

"Tea!" The hermit shouts. "We must have tea to celebrate. Please sit!"

Gage clears small stacks of magazines from two nearby chairs and sits. The wizard shuffles into his kitchen.

"Why are we here?" Gage whispers to Newt above the tinny hiss of water pouring into a tea kettle. Newt stands and walks two short steps over to Gage, sits lightly upon his lap.

"I want to answer your other question first," she says, her warmth snuggling up against him. "No matter what environment you put them in, the birds find a way to evolve their song. Put them in the city—where they compete with the roar of mass traffic and whine of police sirens—and their dialect will adapt to cut through the static. Put them in the ocean, and they modulate the frequency of their calls to carry over the crashing of the waves. Sometimes within the same generation. Can you image that?"

The magician bustles back into the room and settles back into the recliner.

"So you've come for your final wish?" He asks.

Newt smiles at Gage, throwing her arms around his neck to kiss him passionately on the lips.

"Yes," Newt says.

She jumps up from Gage's lap and leans down to whisper in the magician's ear. Gage can hear the first, whistling hints of the tea kettle working itself up to a boil in the other room. The magician smiles then, and nods purposefully at Newt.

With a sound like the pealing of bells, Newt disappears into thin air, leaving behind only the piercing cry of the tea kettle and a few gray feathers, which float slowly down to rest upon the magician's cluttered floor.

For a long time after that Gage wanders, lost, through the ages, haunted by the ancient blood magic coursing thickly through his veins. He seeks refuge in airports, in the comforting drone of jet engines, circling high above the clouds. A need sprouts within him, growing stronger every day: that residual pull from Newt, the old undertow, still stringing him along.

He studies languages, secluding himself in dusty library stacks, hoping to plumb some hidden depth Newt might have overlooked. But Gage finds that the more deeply he delves into the complexities of language, the farther away he drifts from the world and his experiences of it. So he turns his attention to birds: sparrows and night herons, ibis and barnacle geese, cranes, vultures and the common crow.

And then, many hundreds of years later, Gage stumbles upon the magician one last time, playing Chinese poker in a St. Petersburg café for an evening's supply of wine and cigarettes. Gage pulls the man aside, demanding answers.

"I need to know what she wished for," Gage says.

"Why?"

"How did you put it ... what she desired? Above all things? I need to know!"

A tufted brow arches above the magician's good eye. Gesturing for Gage to lean closer, he whistles a fractured melody into his ear: a delicate warble, like the carefree singing of sparrows in springtime.

"What does it mean?"

"Nothing," the magician answers. "It means nothing at all."

The winters in County Down, Northern Ireland, grow shorter with the passing of each season. In the sister cities of Strangford and Portaferry, the locals have noticed that the geese seem to appear later every year. But the warmer days draw more families down to the water, where mothers and fathers stroll the strand sipping hot tea from paper cups, watching their tightly-bundled children frolic in the tide pools.

At the end of a long afternoon spent chasing geese at the edge of the water, the children are often cold, damp, and hungry. After supper and bath, snugly wrapped in their blankets, the children listen to their tired parents tell fairy tales before bed, Celtic stories of sea maidens and stolen children, pale ghosts and massive giants, screaming banshees and the eerily fearsome faerie folk. Few of these are written down; many of them change with each telling.

One story, in particular, has become a bedtime favorite: about a couple both blessed and cursed by an overwhelming need for one another, changelings careening across the continents—sometimes as man and wife, sometimes disguised as birds, sometimes appearing as animals never before seen under the sun. An old hermit living at the edges of Portaferry is rumored to tell the story best, his crooked fingers wiggling in front of an eye clotted with cataracts, as he spins fantastic yarns about the couple's adventures through the ages.

Some say if you're out on the beach before dawn in late winter, you may see the faraway figure of a man walking the beach, calling out to the geese in the half light. If you're lucky, you might also see a bird rise up from the gaggle, winging through the pale pre-dawn fog toward the strand where he stands, waiting. A fisherman boasts he once saw the goose fly right into the man's outstretched arms; for a moment the two of them looked like lovers, locked in a passionate embrace. The fisherman's wife says it was a woman who emerged from the flock, and swears she saw the two of them walking together toward the dunes.

But then the rest of the geese blew by their boat in a flurry, and they lost the couple in the mist as the birds flew north, readying for spring.

# Wade German

Lichfield

When the school bus stopped in Lichfield
a kid would get on. Always a different one.
They all looked like birds in antiquated clothes;
smelled of mold and fresh-turned earth.
They always took back seats, sat there mute.
We never spoke to them, didn't like their town:
green curtains of phantasmal light
draped the narrow rows of old gray houses
like crooked tombstones on a patch of prairie
long since abandoned by normal souls.
Those kids never got off with us, and we never
saw the same one again. They were swallowed
by the cloud of our unknowing. The driver kept mute
on what was further up the road.

Jessica Plattner
Featured Artist Gallery & Profile

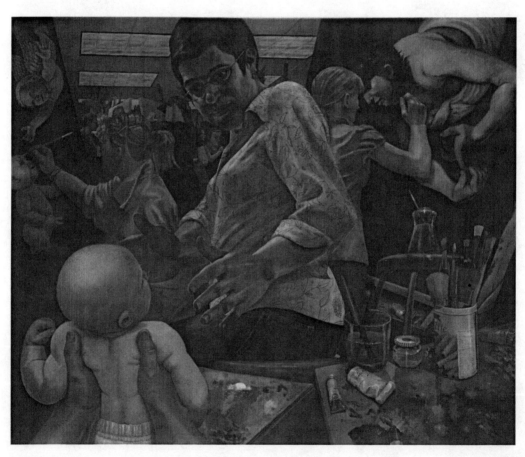

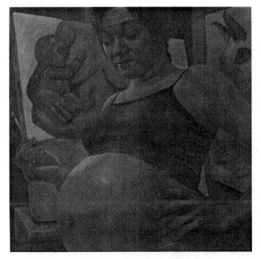

02

03

04

Jessica Plattner

05

05a

06

07

08

09

10

Harmony and the Imagination:
A Conversation with Jessica Plattner

Jodi Varon

"Poets and beggars, musicians and prophets, warriors and scoundrels, all creatures of that unbridled reality, we have had to ask but little of imagination, for our crucial problem has been a lack of conventional means to render our lives believable."
—Gabriel García Márquez, from "The Nobel Lecture."

Jessica Plattner embraces both the worrisome and celebratory unknown with playful fecundity. The future may hold menace, but it also offers sustenance and joy. Consider as example St. Christopher Carrying His Child-Self Across the River, Jessica Plattner's cover painting for the inaugural issue of Phantom Drift. The subject, a monkish St. Christopher waist deep in water, ferries a child across a stream, the child an infant with the wizened head of a man complete with five o'clock shadow.

Plattner's work invites us to read surface and symbols. Each canvas is a complex story, a chapter, a narrative, a resonance within a long and rich mythopoetic tradition of story-telling and painting. Working with an eclectic primary palette and rich patterns reminiscent of Renaissance textiles and tapestries, Plattner's use of divided space and multiple perspectives allows the serious and sublime elbow room for humor and dreams that augment the complex narratives in her work. How would Plattner describe the balance of conception and completion in her painting, and how might the moniker "new fabulist" or the phrase "elements of the fantastic" describe the work included in her most recent portfolio, Fact and Fancy: Narrative Portraits 2009-10, of which St. Christopher Carrying His Child-Self Across the River is a part? The portfolio was unveiled as a solo exhibition at the Common Sense Gallery, Edmonton, Alberta, Canada September 10-October 8, 2010.

Cradling her infant daughter, Sofie, the rich essence of Indian curry permeated Plattner's kitchen as we spoke. A Gibson guitar was close at hand, flanked by packing boxes as Plattner and her partner, Canadian painter and musician, Dean Smale, prepared for Plattner's 2011-12 sabbatical from Eastern Oregon University, where she teaches painting and drawing. Her sabbatical will include studio work in Medicine Hat, Alberta, Canada, and an artist-in-residency in Florence, Italy.

Flux and generation define Plattner's living and workspace now, and, though separated by a spacious second story studio, her canvasses vie with daughter Sofonisba (Sofie) Ann Plattner Smale's more immediate needs and three dimensional play toys of spinning fish, giraffes, and flying bumble bees. Plattner points to a six-plus year obsession with motherhood, and explained, "Even as an undergraduate, I thought about dolls, baby dolls, and the function of dolls in the lives of girls and women."

Many of Plattner's suites, such as the work in Indecision (2005-2006), Sueños (2005-2007), and her Fulbright Scholarship project completed in Guanajuato, Mexico 2007-08, Maternal Instincts: Portraits of Women in Oregon and Mexico challenge conventional views on the saintly mother. In these paintings we encounter surreal, fractured planes, macabre elements, disproportional, looming, unsettling infants. Women mime domesticity while clutching dolls, dogs, or empty space. In Sleeper and Escape, from the Sueños suite (2005-2007), slumbering infants entrust heads, torsos, and legs in the tooth-lined maws of giant carp-like fish whose glistening skin is akin to the prints on tablecloths and flannel pajamas, starkly contrasting with the rich brown hues of the infants' skin. The fish and the innocents remind us of Job's biblical whale and Plattner's consuming urges, her fears of the world of harm awaiting birth. Invoking the domestic ambiguity of German expressionist Otto Dix and his Nelly with Doll II, Plattner's Wallpaper (2005-06) takes up her earlier fascination with dolls along with fantasies about reality and the secret essence of dolls.

One of Plattner's favorite creepy stories is "La muñeca menor" ("The Youngest Doll") by Puerto Rican writer Rosario Ferre, in which the niece of a wounded woman bitten by a prawn transmogrifies into a porcelain-skinned doll with the sounds of the ebbing and rising tides where her heartbeat should be. In Plattner's painting the almost real, larger-than-life doll sits in the lap of an ambivalent and uncomfortable looking Plattner. As portrait subject, her short, flowered sun-dress bunches high on her thighs, her legs covered with grey-hued stockings that stop a few inches above her knees. The doll's red patterned dress and the deep pink wallpaper behind it, printed with daisies and ferns, swirl in a domestic medley checked by the worried look in the woman's doe-eyed gaze. The doll's right hand strokes the woman's face, the doll's flesh too pink and shiny to be "real," to be human. I wondered how Plattner might paint Sofie, given her macabre portrayal of the all-consuming needs of dolls and the children they represent. All Plattner would say is, "I want to paint Sofie all of the time; the color of her skin is outrageous."

Daughter of noted painter Phyllis Plattner and anthropologist Stuart Plattner, Plattner spent part of her childhood in Central America and several years in her early 20s painting and teaching English in San Cristobal de las Casas, Chiapas, Mexico. She credits the daily discipline of her mother's studio work and professional teaching with imbuing her with an artist's habits of mind, and the example of her father's field work sparked her own interest not in ethnology, per se, but in the schooled and questioning way an anthropologist observes people. Living and working in San Cristobal, especially, infused Plattner's palette with the rich, deep colors of tropical fruits and flowers. The primary colors adorning buildings, clothing, and altars resonate in her work. Rhythms of daily life in Mexico and Central America inform the narratives in Plattner's paintings with magic-real dream elements as well as the complex symbols of Mexican socialist-realism, folklore, and religion. Inspired by the art of Frida Kahlo, Plattner folds Kahlo's hues, dreams, meditations, and nightmares into Plattner's own representation of personal meditations, feminism, and motherhood.

By this time in our conversation, Sofie was on her second, restive feeding. Sofie too has deep painters' roots. She is named for Plattner's favorite Renaissance painter, Sofonisba Anguissola (1527-1625). Anguissola shares a similar biography with Plattner—daughter of a well-educated progressive thinker, Anguissola's father educated his daughters and encouraged Anguissola to paint. Apprenticed to the accomplished painter Bernardino Campi, and, painting in the Spanish court of Phillip II, Anguissola was one of the few successful woman painters during the Renaissance. Like Plattner, Anguissola specialized in self-portraits, as self-portraits of women were rare in that period. Plattner recounted an anecdote about Anguissola, how her contemporary Michelangelo saw Anguissola's painting of a crying child and "praised the expression in the baby's expressive face."

As a way to explain her humor and her love of narrative, art history, and multiple perspectives, Plattner shared with me her favorite painting by Anguissola, the surreal and humorous *Bernardino Campi Painting Sofonisba Anguissola* (c. 1559). There are at least three gazes in the painting, and Anguissola tricks us into viewing the artificial perceptions of her subjects. The largest image on the canvas is that of student Sofonisba, wearing a brocade maroon gown with a high, white collar. Her red tresses are smooth and taut, save for the curls at her hairline. The second figure, the austere and serious Bernardino Campi, gazes out, presumably at the painter of the entire canvas, Sofonisba Anguisola.

The portrait-subject Campi is painting, Sofonisba Anguisola, also gazes at the artist, Sofonisba Anguisola. The artist herself presumably gazes at the entire scene while her subjects gaze at her. Predating the Surrealists' juxtaposition of context, gaze, painter and subject by almost 400 years, Anguissola's humor and wry sense of story infuse much of Plattner's work.

Plattner retold the parable of St. Christopher, how he was renowned for his great height, more than seven feet, and how he was asked to ferry an infant across a swiftly flowing stream. As the infant climbed up on St. Christopher's shoulders, the stream picked up velocity, and with each step into the deeper water, the current gained momentum and the infant grew heavier and heavier. Half way across, and in the deepest part of what now seemed a river, the burden was unbearable and St. Christopher thought he would perish amid the waves and foam of the roaring waters, unable to save the life of the child. Despite St. Christopher's doubt, he made the passage safely and discovered that he was ferrying the Christ child across the water.

The allegorical tale vivifies hope and piety, though Plattner had other reasons for choosing St. Christopher as her subject. "I liked the story," she said. "St. Christopher, in addition to being the patron saint of travelers, is also the patron saint of San Cristobal de las Casas, Chiapas, Mexico, where I lived for three years painting and teaching English. Also, I wanted to capture Dean's humor."

Smale, who is the model for St. Christopher, is portrayed in profile as meditative, struggling. He is also portrayed as his infant-self being ferried across the water on St. Christopher's shoulders. Clothed in muted red pajamas, the infant's face is a mirror image of the adult St. Christopher's, and the infant's gaze matches the seriousness of the adult's face with an expression of wisdom and concern far beyond his years. Plattner agreed that portraying Smale as both infant and adult could be interpreted as a magic real element, but as she watched infant Sofie trying to grasp our conversation while Smale searched for his daughter's favorite video, Shaun the Sheep, Plattner remarked on the elusive expression of wisdom on infants' faces. So, then, is the expression on the infant's face in St. Christopher accurate, hyperbolic, magic real? "Maybe all those things," Plattner said, "but my main focus was to capture the moment."

A black bear sits entranced on the nearby bank in Plattner's newest version of the tale, not the grim figure of a hanged man swinging from a gallows as in Hieronymus Bosch's earlier rendition of the allegory, *St. Christopher Carrying the Christ Child*. Plattner's depicted landscape is the watery Pacific Northwest, thick with cattails and

Indian paintbrush, male and female mallards afloat on the water near St. Christopher and the child. The curves in the distant hills are soft, rounded rather than craggy, suggesting cultivation and domesticity rather than the dangerous crags of more inhospitable mountains or an arid, biblical landscape. We see inviting cabins with lighted windows built on green, undulating hills with well-tended paths leading from house to house. Plattner's St. Christopher, supported by a staff in his right hand and left arm outstretched, hand taut, depicts concentration as he balances among slippery river-rocks. The infant on his shoulders is likewise serious, his small body twisted in an uncomfortable posture. Submerged to his waist, the waters surrounding St. Christopher look clear and calm, so glassy the hillsides' green outlines are reflected in the water.

"What is raging rages within the mind of the adult St. Christopher," Platter continued, explaining that one of the painting's narratives, in addition to drawing on the mythic parable of St. Chrisopher, draws on Smale's biography. Plattner explained, "I wanted to depict Dean carrying his own difficult and treacherous childhood on his back across the river, to a shore that has domestic imagery. It's a positive journey. He's crossing over in a literal and figurative sense. I don't want to illustrate the story as it already exists; I want to reveal a bigger story that unfolds in the painting."

"The same goes for dreams," Plattner said, explaining at length:

> Frida Kahlo and the surrealists were great examples of painters using dream elements. Suzanna and the Elders began as a dream. I was in my bed, and the door was high up on the wall, almost to the ceiling, higher than I could reach or climb. There was someone looking down on me from above, peering at me from a window, also high along the wall of the room, almost at the ceiling line as well. I felt trapped, menaced. I tried to paint the dream imagery directly, but I couldn't figure out how to get the perspective of someone looking down from a great height in a threatening way.
>
> I tried building a little model of the room from my dream to understand something about the perspective, but it didn't seem to go anywhere. I did end up using the model as the subject of The Artist's Room, with a baby towering over a small bedroom.
>
> Finally I tried using the system of three point perspective to draw the scene, because with it you can look out and down simultaneously in the

painting. As I worked on the composition, I continued to think about stories, where someone threatening is gazing at someone else, usually a more innocent someone. During the Renaissance, artists loved to paint the biblical story of Suzanna and the Elders, in which creepy old men spy on a beautiful young naked woman bathing in a pond. I decided to tackle the narrative without focusing on the naked body of the woman, but instead on the psychology of the old men. I was using a model from school for the older man's face, and his personal narrative entered the painting similar to the way Dean's personal narrative entered St. Christopher. In my Suzanna and the Elders painting, the model had recently broken up with his long-time partner, and he seemed really sad and separated from his home life. The model wasn't a threatening man, but I liked him for this painting because he was so filled with longing.

The man in Plattner's Suzanna and the Edlers, his size exaggerated, gazes down from a dream-like height into a jazzy bathroom with lavender wallpaper, a bathtub full of frothy bubbles on the right-hand side of the canvas. At first we see what seems to be an empty room and wonder at the man's sad curiosity. Or is it prurience? On closer inspection the form of a girl with a long blonde braid, wearing a red and white polka-dotted bathrobe is reflected in the bathroom mirror. Presumably Suzanna, the girl seems unaware of her stalker, as she is about to take a bubble bath. Plattner paints the scene as less physically menacing than the Renaissance painter, Artemisia Gentileschi's rendition of the tale. Gentileschi, a contemporary of Sofonisba Anguissola, depicts the encroaching rape of Suzanna and the carnality of the perpetrators much more visibly. The huge presence of the stalker peering in the high window in Plattner's rendition of the story has no less deep psychological impact, but several narratives suggest themselves at once in Plattner's painting: potential menace; the self-loathing the stalker seems to project; the bather unaware of the man's presence, the man's fingertips pressed hard against the window's glass, and our helpless witness to the scene. The high window's perspective implicates entrapment of both the girl and us.

"I think of Suzanna in the biblical story as innocent too," Plattner said. "The old men were suspect and lustful. Suzanna was just bathing. The sin was in their hearts, not hers."

Nobel laureate Gabriel García Márquez, in the epigraph to this piece, chafes at European descriptions of Central and South America—descriptions of fantastical flora and fauna, descriptions of natives rendered foolish and child-like, descriptions of slaughter and the lust for gold. He challenges the nomenclature "magic realism" used to describe his masterwork One Hundred Years of Solitude and cites the "outsized reality" experienced by the peoples of Central and South America, of massacres, dictatorships, disappearances, the "furtively adopted children" born of Argentine women incarcerated during that country's infamous dictatorship in the 1970s. He says his work is not exaggeration, but truthful. "We put too many checks on ourselves," Plattner says, referencing imagination. "But I don't set out to make something weird or offbeat or fantastical, and I think that's what García Márquez is saying as well." She ended our conversation with this observation:

> Part of painting is just a technical challenge. I remember getting in an argument with a professor in grad school while we were in the Metropolitan Museum of Art in New York. We were looking at the Courbet painting, Woman with a Parrot, and he said 95% of painting is just technical challenges, just labor. I did not like that idea, because I felt that the content of a painting has to be more important than 5% of it, that the ideas and the story itself are more important. But now, the longer that I've been painting, when I think of my own painting process, I'd say that 98% of the process is technical challenges. For example, how do I make purple and yellow, two complimentary colors, work harmoniously in a painting? How am I going to do that? That's what I think about. It's those kinds of technical challenges that I'm mostly thinking about. Then it's the content I end up talking about all the time, but it's not really what guides the process of painting.

List of Plates

Cover Art: "St. Christopher Carrying his Child-self Across the River," oil on linen, 2009, 45" X 48"

01   "The Art Teacher's Premonition," oil on linen, 2010, 48" X 60"
Description: This self-portrait tells the story of a dream I had the night before I found out I was pregnant. In the dream I find myself in a busy painting studio surrounded by productive students. Suddenly someone hands me a baby to watch, forcing me to reconsider my roles as woman, teacher, and artist.

02   "Expecting," oil on linen, 2010, 24" X 24"
Description: I completed this painting a few days before my daughter was born. In it I am contemplating the surreal transformation of my body, while questioning the future changes in my artistic production.

03   "The Artist's Room," oil on linen, 2010, 24" X 18"
Description: One of the last paintings completed during my pregnancy, this image shows a baby towering over a small bedroom. I want to express my wonder and apprehension at the disproportionate power of a baby in a parent's life.

04   "Leda and the Swan (The Taxidermist)," oil on linen, 2009, 36" X 60"
Description: In the original myth, Leda is seduced by Zeus in the form of a swan. The model for this painting, a tough-minded creative young woman from Alaska, turns the table on the swan.

05   "Suzanna and the Elders," oil on linen, 2010, 48" X 45" (05a -- detail)

06   "Escape," oil on canvas, 2006, 24" X 36"

07   "Encounter," oil on canvas, 2006, 16" X 24"

08   "Wallpaper," oil on canvas, 2006, 24" X 18"

09   "Sketch (dissection)," ballpoint pen, watercolor and collage on paper, 2006, 10" X 8"

10   "Abundance (detail)," charcoal, acrylic, and collage on paper, 2006, 40" X 30"

11   "The Hungry Ghost," oil on linen, 2007, 40" X 30"
Description: In Tibetan Buddhism, the "hungry ghost" is a figure with a ravenous appetite but a tiny neck, making eating impossible. The woman depicted here uses this concept in her yoga practice as an antidote to years of struggling with eating disorders.

12   "sketches for work in progress," collage, 2011
Description: These are sketches of possible subjects for a piece I'm developing on Cupid (the Roman god, not today's Valentine's Day cherub) and his mother Venus.

For more information on Jessica Plattner's art, visit her website at: **www.jessicaplattner.com**

Peter Grandbois
What the Billy Goat Said

*I On the Relative Uncertainty of Possible Worlds,
   or How to Remember the Future.*

    The Billy Goat stands beside your bed, resting his head in the crook of your neck. His dirty brown fur is matted; his golden eyes dull. Those sideways slits staring.

    You notice one horn is longer than the other and think how odd. But odder still is the green garter around the Billy Goat's neck with a bell attached to it and the ace bandage on his left front leg, where, you suppose, his knee would be.

    You roll over and try to go back to sleep, to forget about his horns poking into the back of your neck. You don't like goat eyes, never have. It's not that they're demonic. Rather, it's like staring into holes in your own imperturbable reality. You pull the sheets over your head. You pray he's gone, hoping he went in search of oats or ivy, whatever it is goats eat. His warm breath caresses your back. He's under there with you. You're sure of it.

    What if you knew? the Billy Goat asks, kicking you in the shin with his hoof. Would you still wear those white shirts each and every day? Would you still fight to keep them clean?

    Before you know it, you're dressed in your finest black suit, the one in the back of the closet you save for weddings and funerals. He's prodding you with his horns, shoving you out the door.

    Don't leave home without the red slippers! the Billy Goat shouts. No, not *those* red slippers. The other ones. You know, the ones with the embroidered gold dragons, the ones your mother bought when you were five. Yes, we all need our red slippers if we want to slip,

slip,

slip

    You want to tell him you don't know what he's talking about. But, you do, don't you? You know exactly where he's going.

The corpse-blue cart is topped with a leopard skin seat, quite plush, though the wheels are on fire. The Billy Goat harnesses himself, then, with a ringing of his bell, limps along, pulling you behind him.

II   *Should a Materialist Believe in Reduction of Experience, or How to Clear out the Furniture of the Mind?*

I can see by your mother's picture in the locket you wear around your neck that she didn't tell you everything. Oh yes, she told you to behave, to be kind, like all good little boys, but did she say your fingers were getting longer, the knuckles like knots twisting and pretzling until someday squirrels would crawl upon your hands, nest in your ears?

The moon flips overhead. The sun licks the horizon. Your house sits on the corner, a flagstone path leading to the door. Flowers line the porch. Birds chirp. Trees grow. It's all so pretty. *Is that how it was?* you want to ask, but the Billy Goat does all the talking.

Look! he exclaims, as he pulls you past the scene. There you are, riding your skateboard, practicing three-sixties in the driveway. Careful, or you'll fall and break your arm!

(Oh, I'm sorry. That was a nasty crash.)

You lie in the driveway, crying. Your skateboard hides beneath the neighbor's hedge. Mother emerges from the house, wraps you in her long arms, and the sky is all bubbles—pink, orange, yellow and blue.

She takes you by the hand, points out tulips and hyacinths, robins and bunnies.

Can I name them? you hear yourself ask. Happy to please her. Happy to know.

By all means, the Billy Goat says, limping noticeably now. Our first dream memory is that of naming. Do you remember? The bunny you called, *Frau Biebel,* the flowers, *so sorry,* and of course, your first pets, the hermit crabs: *Stay Away,* and *Be My Friend!*

What are names for?

They're what keep you from seeing when you look at things.

You let go of your mother's hand and climb the cottonwood next to the stream that runs behind your house.

Listen to the birds, the Billy Goat shouts to the boy that you were. Listen, as you swing from branch to branch. But you don't listen. Instead, you dream of soft, damp holes, holes that hide you, holes that grow teeth. *Mother get off me. I'm grown now!*

Frau Biebel cowers behind a tree. Blood streaks her white fur, as she tears out chunks of her arm. Still you dream on.

A tunnel, long and dark. Your bare feet squish down through mud. You light match after match, but only shadows of rats flicker along the walls. Look, there's your father standing in the driveway next to his Buick. See how he shoves his clothes into the trunk. The way the trunk bounces back open because he slams it too hard. Run if you like, the Billy goat says, but watch out for the glass buried in the mud. It will only slice those tender feet.

The faster you run, the more you sink. Until, just before the mud swallows you, your father's car pulls out of the driveway.

Too late, the Billy Goat whispers in your ear. You're the head of the family now.

Stay Away and *Be My Friend* hide in their shells. *Frau Biebel* scampers down a hole.

Bubbles drip, DRIP, DRIP in the west, distorting our pleasant picture.

The specific gravity of knowledge is greater than water, the Billy Goat says. Do yourself a favor and throw it away. His eyes narrow until he looks almost human. Let go and you'll float to the surface.

You dig your long, stick fingers into the dirt on either side of the cart.

Your roots aren't deep enough, he continues.

You fling a fist full of earth in the Billy Goat's face.

Oh, I see, he replies, wiping off the dirt with his hoof. You want more.

III Proof Concerning the Subliminal Necessity for Quantity in the Face of Determinate Annihilation.

Give me Lucky Charms, Cheerios, Count Chocula and Frankenberry. Give me Elvis Presley: Aloha From Hawaii, The Beach Boys: Surfin' Safari, give me the official Evel Knieval doll, give me Gordon and Smith boards with lime-green Kryptonite wheels and Tracker Trucks, give me the Bushnell Deep Space Scope, give me Atomic Skis with diagonal release bindings, give me The Clash: London Calling, give me a '69 Plymouth, give me an Apple, then later a Sony, then a Dell, then back to Apple, lose the Plymouth, give me a Daihatsu, a Honda, a Toyota, Jeep, Toyota, Ford, and finally a Subaru. Give me the national fencing title, give me the Olympic team, give me fame, give me a poem in a magazine, no make that a story, a book!

IV The World as Weakness of Will, or On the Demerits of Filth: an Axiom Supporting the Maxim "Cleanliness is next to Godliness."

Dooby-dooby-doo, Exchanging glances, dooby-dooby-doo What were the chances...
Damn that crooner! the Billy Goat cries. Always horning in!
As the smooth, seductive sound floats closer, you note another noise, that of a spring bouncing, then retracting, followed by a scraping over rock.
A spotlight shines on a giant black cat dressed in a white dinner jacket with a black bow tie. Quite dapper! He holds a radio microphone from the fifties, which he keeps close to his mouth whenever he sings. A Jack-in-the-box bounces and drags itself up behind the cat. Jack's pushing your bed with one hand; the other hand is outstretched, wobbling invitingly.
Scotty-watty-dum, Foh deedle dum dum.
Don't listen to him, the Billy Goat says.
But, you can't help it. The sound intoxicates, like the smell of honey toast in the morning.
And don't look into Jack's tired eyes, the Billy Goat continues. They've seen the shifting shapes beneath your bed, the gibbering mouths in your closet. He's taken their names, swallowed them whole. Why do you think he's so blue?
It's not the eyes that draw your attention. It's your image reflecting back to you from Jack's top hat, an image distorted as if the hat were a fun house mirror. The image calls to you, a small squeak of a voice, and as you step closer, you realize the voice is your own. It's getting louder:
"You surfer of Internet porn, riding over firm, young bodies! You masturbator in dark rooms!"
"Daddy can you play?"
"Not now, I'm working."
Yes, Jack says. I see the bar of soap in your hands. Do you want me to clean you?
If only it were so easy, kid. From behind the microphone, Captain Cool winks.
"You tearless mourner at funerals! You envious brother! You loser of friends, rings and wives, of skin, hair and desire!"
Do you like that? Dooby Doo. Captain Cool steps in so close you can smell his aftershave. *Cartier. Scum ditty wadda doo doo, do you?*
Jack reaches out his wobbly hand. Take it, Captain Cool says. *Titty watta coo, doo dahbee take it.* We don't have all day, kid. *Just tah tah dee dahbee dah take it.* Come, little

valentine...come live...my funny valentine... right in the center of your dirty, little mah mah doo daddy wah monkey mind.

You reach out your hand.

That's when the Billy Goat lowers his head and charges. You have to admit you didn't think he had it in him, the way he limped around like that. But now he's all Billy Goat gumption, knocking Jack head over box. Of course, Captain Cool escapes, slips out the back, unscathed, not a spot of dirt on him. His voice echoes in the distance: *Although I may be the cat some girls think of as handsome...*

You climb onto the Billy Goat's back, and he bounds through dripping paint skies. A tear of blood trickles from beneath the ace bandage on the Billy Goat's leg.

V How to Arrive at the Simplicity Injunction, or Knowing without Knowing

There are holes, you'd swear there are holes. Black patches everywhere on the deep blue. Holes with great eyes peeking through. Holes that lead to the center of things, to names and what's behind them. The forest is thick; the leafless branches reach out.

Unfurl your fingers, the Billy Goat says, *fling your monkey self into every tree!*

And you do. You rip monkeys from your thigh, your groin, your shoulder and your head and hurl them to the trees. They chitter angrily demanding you take them back. The Billy Goat is hobbling now, his bandaged leg almost useless.

Throw your monkey mind to the flames!

Uncertain, you look about. The only flames you see rage from the wheels of the Billy Goat's cart.

Why are you waiting? he asks. *Don't you see the flames?*

And, as if the word conjured the flames themselves, you do. The holes in the sky burn, thousands of incendiary eyes. You wipe your hand on your jacket afraid your sweat will prevent you from getting a good grip.

It's your choice.

Your long, knotted fingers pull at the last shreds of your hair, peel back your scalp. You hesitate, your mind quivering in your palm.

Don't forget, the Billy Goat says as he unhooks himself from the harness. *To become infinite you must pare yourself down, cut away the flesh, gnaw at the muscle, snap the sinew and dissolve the bone.*

You cast your mind to the flames, and, together, you watch it burn.
I'd forgotten there were birds. So many birds.

VI The Necessity of Diligence, Precision and Other Conceits

Well done! the Billy Goat says as he offers you his hoof.

The throbbing in your temples is gone. The sun shines. Where there were once holes, starfish hang from the sky in infinite variety. Chirping sounds from every tree.

Don't forget the cat on your back, the Billy Goat warns.

"Thank God," you say. "It was only a murmur. Life a mere murmur."

The birdsong surrounds you until you're standing inside it.

And, don't forget to tinder your mind in the flames, the Billy Goat says before hobbling away.

"I'm sorry?" you say. "I didn't catch that."

But listen, Captain Cool's crooning in the distance, *Doo waddy dooby doo daa.* Jack's squeaking and scratching provides the counterpoint.

The cock cries for us all, Jack says, when he arrives.

Too true, bah booty boo, Captain Cool agrees. And then he launches into his next little ditty, leaning in close, tickling you with his whiskers as he sings.

VII Does God Have to Exist? or Why You'll "Never Walk Alone"

"Just a minute. I need to take a pee," you say.

No problem, kid, Captain Cool replies. Jack's head bobs wildly.

You run through the wasteland, desperate for a place to hide. A lone outhouse stands on the horizon, dogs playing in front of the door.

You hold your breath and enter. Dropping your pants, you sit on the cold wood seat, not worrying about splinters, telling yourself to forget about what lies deep in the hole below, not to mention spiders under the lid. *Don't cry. Damn it!* You hold your breath until the outhouse walls spin around you, then gag on the stench.

Hurry it up there, kid, the voice of Captain Cool calls from right outside the door.

"Just a minute," you say, grabbing a reader's digest, turning desperately to the article on *Fire Hazards in the Home.*

I know it's no picnic, kid, Captain Cool whispers through the door. But I gotta tell ya, when I get down, I just sing a little tune and pretty soon things start looking up.

Me me me me me. Captain Cool begins his vocal warm up.

Come on, Jack says. It's easy.

Moo moo moo moo moo. Can't stress the importance of vocal warm ups, kid.

Slowly, you open the door. Peek out.

That's it, Jack continues. Just follow the sound of the Captain's voice, and remember, if you get tired, I'm here to help. No need to exert yourself.

Jack flops his wobbly arm over your shoulder.

> *When you walk through a storm*
> *Always wear your best hat*
> *And don't be afraid of the sun.*
> *For, at the end of the storm is the Monkey King*
> *And the sweet, silver straps of his chair*

You feel better already. Captain Cool can carry a tune.

Here, let me strap a bible to each foot, Jack says. You'll need something to keep the fire away.

> *Walk on through the wind,*
> *Walk on through the rain,*
> *Tho' your dreams be tossed and blown.*

Just keep looking up. Do you see him now? There, in that fluffy, white cloud. Do you see His radiant face smiling down? Gives me goose bumps every time.

> *And you'll never walk alone,*
> *You'll never, ever walk alone.*

VIII   On the Phenomenology of Physical Discomfort,
       Or, Why a Good Dentist is Hard to Find

Willkommen...zit in my chair. I've been vaiting. Relax. I'm not dat kind of King. Now, open vide. Ya. Let me get good look.

It can be painful, ya. Tell me vhen it hurts, and I give you dis oil. Cloves can be very comforting. Pain und pleasure. Pain und pleasure. Dat's vhat makes da vorld go 'round.

The Monkey King's furry fingers dig in your mouth. It hurts so bad you want to scream. So, with eyes wide, you nod your head as if you'd consented to this in the first place. The Monkey King smiles as He works. His teeth are yellow and rotting.

You've got tree millimeters of gum recession. Vhat's da mattah, don't you floss?

You're choking slowly on your own blood.

Ach! Dis apron is ruined. I better change it. Here, take dis vater and rinse vhile I'm gone.

Captain Cool smiles winningly as he looks on. Jack's head swings from side to side approvingly. They know it's for the best. The Monkey King returns, examining your X-ray.

As I suspected, dat tooth is rotten. It vill have to come out! Hold still now, dis von't hurt a bit. A little shot of painkiller. Ya. Der you go. It only hurts when I viggle da needle. Keep dat mouth open. Vide. Vider. Gut. Gut.

He raises His furry hand, the pliers gleaming in the afternoon sun. Then He bends over you. The light goes out.

Dat's it. I've got it. Ein, zwei, drei...

Green grass stretches before you. Captain Cool stands ready, microphone in hand. Jack's smiling face bobs up and down.

Where are the birds?

Gehen sie. It vas just a rotten tooth, the Monkey King says, patting your back. Don't vorry about da dark clouds gathering. Pretend you don't zee dem. Und remember, if you need me, I'm here vith my pliers, my probes, my drill.

Captain Cool slides his arm around you...*There's somebody I'm longing to see. I hope that He turns out to be.* Jack hops along behind. *Someone to watch over me.*

The grass is cool under your bare feet. It all seems so lovely. It doesn't matter that there aren't any birds, does it?

Don't mind da murmuring, the Monkey King shouts, a speck in the distance now. Dey are always murmuring like dat. Murmur, murmur goes da little stream of voices forever und ever.

Carolyn Ives Gilman
Dwindle Chick

Her first meeting, she must have topped 275. Everything was big: her laugh, her boobs, her chins, her energy for life. She was going to tackle the weight tiger, she said with that chesty voice and oversized confidence. Her goal was to lose 150. None of us thought she could do it.

She always carried a canvas book bag stuffed with volumes like Rabelais and Roethke. Our counselor said, "Girl, this is too heavy. You've got to *lose* the weight, not take it on."

She needed intervention. First we taught her to lighten up her conversation—more reality shows and cosmetics, lose the Social Issues. We edited all that highbrow jazz and fusion music off her Ipod. She was weighed down with art film knowledge, all those ten-pound words and leaden metaphors. It had to go. Her laptop was five pounds lighter after we wiped the bookmarks.

As the pounds started to melt, she said her boyfriend was unhappy. He was an NPR-elitist type who said she was "losing substance." He called her "a lightweight" as if it were an insult.

"Dump him!" we all shouted in unison. "He's holding you back!"

And oh how she needed to pare down her expectations for love. She didn't need to carry a soulmate with an intellect like an anchor around her neck. She could be playing the field, urban free, like the paper umbrella without the drink. It wasn't even a sacrifice.

In the end, she reduced herself to a wisp. Minus all that excess personality, she seemed younger by years, like the girl she'd been before the heavy memories. She was svelte and airy, light as a plastic grocery bag in the wind.

How we envied her.

 # Anita Sullivan

When Solstice is Late
(after an old Welsh legend)

One window blackens
the side of a yellow house
on the side of a hill,
the other four still blinded. This window
has moved into place behind
the twisted branches
of our backyard oaks. Floats.
An ancient dowager sits up there sipping tea
and peering with rheumy eyes into the mote-less afternoon;
she watches for the horse, who has not returned.

The horse is late,
sent out to fetch the sun
five days ago, the sun
to ride his back, an impossible thing.

Nobody believes this any more, although
a single window will always appear,
of a blackness unlike
the lightless sides of the stones that shore up the fallow seeds,
unlike the oak-branch silhouettes riddled with sky-holes—
all soft, soft, all postponement, all squandered heart.
Our obsidian gash, our ash from the mouth of night
hangs halfway up the hill, and waits.

For our bone-ridden horse, the unequal one
who goes along the road
his head a wheeled thing.
Who staggers illy
over the horizon, whom
the sun will drop, and flee.

 Matt Schumacher

Exploring The Haunted Palace:
Gothic Warped Space, Phantasmagoria, and The Evolution of the Haunted House from Poe to Danielewski

> *And travelers now within that valley,*
>   *Through the red-litten windows, see*
> *Vast forms that move fantastically*
>   *To a discordant melody;*
> *While, like a rapid, ghastly river,*
>   *Through the pale door,*
> *A hideous throng rush out forever,*
>   *And laugh—but smile no more.*
>
> —Edgar Allan Poe, "The Haunted Palace"

Gaston Bachelard has written that the space of the house "constitutes a body of images that give mankind proofs or illusions of stability." During his classic *The Poetics of Space*, the French phenomenologist defines the house as a sanctuary and shelter that protects that most essential act and agency of human imagination: the formation of the poetic image. Bachelard's house, a bastion of psychic intimacy whose spaces guard our leisurely freedom to dream, has proven especially vulnerable to invasion and disturbance in the literary genre of the ghost story. As Terry Castle asserts in *The Female Thermometer*, phantasmagorical spaces multiply ghosts, allowing them to invade two spaces at once; consequently, specters may simultaneously assail both the house and the mind. Gothic castles and mansions, for instance, with their mad Manfreds and Ambrosios, traditionally disturb and undermine the stability Bachelard ascribes to the house, and become ill-tempered mansions more akin to Poe's haunted palace. Such fictions supplant the Bachelardian poetic image with phantasmagoria, and "warp" the psychic space of the house, according to the terminology of Anthony Vidler. Phantasmagoria and warped space thus function to nightmarishly alter and subvert the very interiority Bachelard posits.

This paper will explore the warped spaces and phantasmagorias of the haunted house in Poe's seminal "The Fall of the House of Usher" and the modern experimentalist haunted suburban gothic abode of Mark Z. Danielewski's *House of Leaves*. I will argue that the immeasurable uncanny dimensions of the American haunted house, introduced by the allegorical, dreamlike dwelling of Poe's groundbreaking tale in the nineteenth century, have grown and warped purposefully during the last hundred and fifty years, to showcase a haunted house more spatiotemporally representative of modern fears. A host of phobias and anxieties Vidler cites as consequences of modernity warp space in *House of Leaves* (including Karen Green's claustrophobia and Johnny Truant's agoraphobia). Among other trepidations looms the notion of the city growing uncontrollably, as if it were a dread and deadly disease. This deviant, inescapable, subversive version of urbanity, whose runaway surfaces, multi-dimensionality, and bewildering multiplicity are unable to be "read" and defy comprehension by any sort of expert, also subvert the mastery of architectural blueprint or urban plan. Thus, a terrible urbanity pursues the Navidson family to the suburbs. Danielewski's modern haunted habitation bespeaks the fear of a city of nothingness so sprawling and invasive that it has not only intruded upon and threatened to ruin the suburbs, but has floated above the blueprint to re-enter(and perhaps re-inter) the suburbanite mind. Furthermore, *House of Leaves* suggests an impossibly bleak and empty dystopian city or an anti-Corbusian chaos-machine. This house presents the sense that urban progress has been little more than illusion. It suggests that all our designs and plans are spectral—that they will return to haunt us and may lead ultimately to nothingness. Lastly, a truly invisible specter haunts Danielewski's postmodernist house, an entity representing the most threatening forces of modernity, forces which, Marshall Berman writes, "threaten(s) to destroy everything we have, everything we know, and everything we are." While Poe's house haunts through authorial use of nineteenth-century brand of phantasmagoria, phantasmagorias have invaded the foundation and walls of Danielewski's modern palace of horrors. The failure of materialism, visible in the crumbling, ruinous exterior of Poe's House of Usher, has warped space to become in Danielewski's dizzying labyrinthine house a vast and rapidly expansive *horror vacui*, an emptiness which reveals, among other things, the failures of the modern American narrative and the modern American dream.

Poe and Phantasmagoria: The Archetypal American Haunted House

"The Fall of the House of Usher" is considered the quintessential early American literary blueprint for the haunted house. In *The Architectural Uncanny*, Anthony Vidler refers to the House of Usher as the "paradigmatic haunted house"(18). Poe's innovative tale unseated the revenant as ghostly intermediary—no small alteration, as the ghost was perhaps the most forceful trope in the more traditional equation of the "elegant nightmare," or English ghost story. The sentient House of Usher and its frightful architectural structure confiscated the ghost's central role, and erected its own architecture of the supernatural. A familiar entity that simultaneously estranges, the House of Usher delivers a more all-encompassing dose of the Freudian uncanny than any otherworldly specter ever could have: this version of the uncanny warps space, expanding to contain and entirely envelop the narrative. Apart from Roderick Usher, the "proprietor," with whom readers likely fail to sympathize despite his ill-health and capacity for delusion, the characters, including the nameless narrator, are less important to the story than the house itself. A family home for many successive generations, the mouldering Usher mansion, with its zigzag crack, "eyelike windows," and as Darrel Abel asserts, "the perilous decrepitude of its constituent materials," displays a portraiture of gloom and disrepair. Moreover, the mansion's exterior has warped to simulate the countenance and fragile intellect of the estate's profoundly troubled owner, Roderick Usher. Critics such as Abel find the zigzag crack in the estate indicative of the precarious state of Usher's health and sanity, as well as his "incoherence and inconsistency." Its "vacant and eyelike windows" bear a more than passing resemblance to Usher's eye, "large, liquid, and luminous beyond comparison," a "luminousness" that, later in the tale, evaporates.

Poe's interiors reveal an even more warped spatiality. "The Fall of the House of Usher," like most of the author's narratives, occurs almost entirely indoors—in this case, within the circuitous, winding corridors and staircases of the Usher mansion. Such an internal arrangement exerts an unusual narratological pressure on the interior, a pressure that threatens to bend or warp space. Dark draperies obscure the walls, and a heavy "air of irredeemable gloom" pervades. Despite this interior pressure, "The Fall of the House of Usher" delivers a plot wrought with indeterminacy, as if the house disallows conventional narrative heroism or progression. In a sense, as Dennis Pahl has written, "the narrator's whole journey, both the physical journey and the verbal one, is a series of mad lines, tracks or passageways that twist and turn (as can be expected in the labyrinthine depths of the

Usher house), leading to nowhere in particular—or at least to no final goal"(10). Richard Wilbur, attentive to the "weird, magnificent," "rich, and eclectic" furnishings of Poe's rooms, furnishings representative "of all periods and all cultures," and "suggestive of great wealth," argues, in a manner not disimilar to Bachelard, that Poe's house is posed as the allegorical dreamscape of the poetic mind. Such an allegory would help corroborate Poe's consistent retreat from reality, and his avoidance of the burgeoning urban condition which surrounded him. It would also help explain the author's penchant for the otherworldly illumination of his interiors—all but impervious or unwilling to readily admit any glint but dim, "feeble gleams of encrimsoned light."

"The Fall of the House of Usher" registers much originality in its manipulation of space and border through phantasmagoria. According to Terry Castle, Edgar Allan Poe "used the phantasmagoria figure precisely as a way of destabilizing the ordinary boundaries between inside and outside, mind and world, illusion and reality"(160). "In (The Fall of the House of)Usher," Castle continues, "one of Roderick Usher's most powerfully 'phantasmagoric' notions—his belief that his dead sister is really alive—far from being illusory, is grotesquely realized when Madeline Usher returns, spectrelike, from the crypt in which she has been interred"(161). Indeterminate boundaries such as these help Poe elasticize space and time. Figures such as Ligeia or Madeline Usher seem to walk through portals created by such warped spaces; uncategorizable, dead and alive, they are dream figures walking to and from the waking world of the visible.

Warped space also arises since Poe may be considered a master of the trope of the downspiral or vortex. Before he descends into the space of the house, our nameless narrator must first stare down into the void of the tarn. More than the traditional crumbling ruin of gothic novels such as Walpole's *The Castle of Otranto*, which houses moral transgressions and cursed ancestries, the House of Usher is a destabilized space, a maelstrom with walls, floor, and ceilings which marshal Roderick and Madeleine Usher to ruin. Richard Fusco, in his study of the inverted helix plot pattern of Maupassant's supernatural madman narratives, could uncover a similar funnel cloud plot pattern operative in Poe's short stories, and in his only novel, *The Narrative of Arthur Gordon Pym*. Space, bent and sent spinning like a whirlpool, perpetually imperils safety, sanity, and empiricism. Seldom does Poe's downspiralling plot not lower the protagonist into doom.

As modernist authors and philosophers such as Nietzsche would propose in the coming twentieth century, the nineteenth century haunted use of Poe, with its definitive fissure, upholds the sign of the troubled split between spiritual and corporeal. Roderick

Usher, the proprietor of dreams, relies on Madeleine for his senses. Without her presence as guide, Roderick, "cadaverously wan," and increasingly subject to fits of "hysteria," succumbs to the "wild influences of his fantastical yet impressive superstitions." Roderick Usher's conception of space and time bends. He appears to perceive stimuli beyond the earthly paradigm of space and time, and ultimately, he retires instead to an otherworldly realm. Poe invited dream and reality to coexist in his haunted house, and he bridged the split between the two through his use of warped space and phantasmagoria.

The Postmodernist Haunted House: Mark Danielewski's House of Leaves

House of Leaves is the most complex, multi-layered, experimental narrative since Poe to locate itself in the genre of the American haunted house tale. One of its most superlative virtues is its ability to bend genres: it is simultaneously considered, for instance, a satire of critical scholarship, a mass-produced artist's book, and a horror novel. On another level, assuredly, the novel may be read as a suburban gothic, during which the fears of the urban condition—confrontations with the Other, poverty, dispossession, estrangement, and baffling multiplicity--all reconvene and pursue the would-be suburbanite to his home skirting the city. Any investigator who consults Bernice Murphy's list of suburban gothic binary oppositions quickly discerns that *House of Leaves* is "haunted," "a place of entrapment and unhappiness," "a claustrophobic breeding ground for dysfunctionality and abuse," and "a place in which the most dangerous threats come from within, not without." In addition to these attributes, the vacuous emptiness stereotypically assigned to the suburbs ironically develops inside the house, taking on, of course, a far more life-threatening form.

A brief summary of the story contained in the novel may avail the uninitiated reader in understanding Danielewski's convoluted haunted house, as well as its multidimensional narrative.

Will Navidson, Pulitzer Prize and Guggenheim-Fellowship-winning photographer, his wife, ex-model Karen Green, and their two children, Chad and Daisy, depart from the city to suburban Williamsburg, Virginia, in a final effort to rescue their "foundering" marriage and reinvigorate their family. Karen has given Navidson an ultimatum: in order to save his marriage, he must abandon his obsessive working habits and refocus on family and marital affairs. Navidson compromises. He decides to make a documentary film of the family, "a record of how Karen and I bought a small house in the country and moved into it with our children"(Danielewski 8). Upon the family's return from a trip to the city of Seattle, Navidson discovers that the house has transformed during their absence. Chad and Daisy have happened upon a new addition: an inexplicable hallway. Navidson ascertains that the house measures larger on the inside than the outside. The house compiles inexplicable and wild additions: a sudden hallway in the living room, a gigantic "spiral staircase," an "endless corridor," doors that suddenly materialize, and other discontinuously shifting, warped architectures. Navidson invites his brother and friend for a look, then hires a team of explorers to investigate. Five explorations into the strange environment ensue. The explorers, among other things, discover through carbon-dating that the material from the walls, "uniformly black with a slightly ashen hue," originates before the solar system.

Danielewski renovates the haunted house to accommodate more contemporary fears of modernity and post-modernity. Neither Poe's allegory of the poetic mind nor the Bachelardian space of the house founds this modern haunted house, where traditional space has been warped by a nightmare interior that defamiliarizes what is at the heart of human self-identity and imagination. If Corbusier's functionalist aphorism that a house should be a *machine*—that is, a space highly streamlined, controlled, and structured to render more efficient, productive living—were applied in this context, Danielewski's house functions as an anti-modernity machine, not unlike Jean Tinguely's self-destructing sculptures, or Mark Pauline's dangerous mechanical exercises in detournement. It is a post-modern structure which generates purposelessness and chaos, that heightens obsession, and leads to abyss, that dismantles and obliterates modernist identity. The gates of its pages and its spurious doors lead to a pastoral gone awry, to a sense of Heideggerian homelessness and dystopia.

As a thematic expectation, readers who survey a suburban gothic tale should not be surprised when the worst of the urban condition materializes to haunt the "bucolic refuge" of the suburban utopia. Impoverishment haunts the Navidson house both psychologically and literally, and manifests itself as reality. The poverty or starvation of love between Will, Karen, and their children, driven by absence, as well as true physical hunger, introduced by confusion within the labyrinth, pursues the Navidson family to the suburbs. Perhaps a hint of the fear inspired by the twentieth century city—the turn-of-the-century poverty of what Peter Hall calls "The City of Dreadful Night," or the end-of-the-century poverty Hall characterizes as "The City of the Permanent Underclass—"

relocates to Navidson's Williamsburg address. The constantly shifting, warped additions to the house open up spaces of menacing darkness like those so feared in the first urban cities. These warped spaces vary the environment, and space and time so greatly that it is impossible to gauge or prepare for the trip into the house, to pack the proper allocation of provisions. All who enter the labyrinthine basement are inevitably threatened with starvation and dehydration. Successful, award-winning Will Navidson, in his plan to live the American dream, nearly starves to death in the labyrinth of his own house. More than any other image, the photograph which won Navidson his Pulitzer haunts and troubles him. It is a photo of "Delial," a Sudanese girl whose picture he took, advancing his photography career just moments before she starved to death.

The fear of disease, evidenced by hygienic campaigns perpetrated by urban planners like Corbusier, rears its bandaged head in the house. The same sense of dread disease that spreads throughout Poe's House of Usher also spreads through *House of Leaves*. In Poe's story, the family physician sneaks past the narrator on the stairs, wearing a "mingled expression of low cunning and perplexity." This is the family physician's only cameo, and his conspiratorial incompetence only heightens the possibility of fatality and affliction. Roderick and Madeleine Usher suffer from an unnameable sickness whose exterior symptoms Poe carefully describes through his observant and sensorily acute narrator: delusional mental instability, pallor, anxiety, and hysteria number a minor record of its symptoms. *House of Leaves*, however, seems imbued with the influence of modern medicine, which can delve under the skin and investigate bodily interiors. Modern medical diagnosis of Danielewski's haunted house, then, might conclude this house is subject to random and deleterious mutation, or victim to rapidly growing, mysterious tumors, as if afflicted with cancer. In Poe's haunted house, readers are allowed to gaze at the exterior symptoms and render their own personal conclusions, but in Danielewski's house, where space is warped by modernity, and here specifically, by modern medicine and its advancements, the reader walks through the disease itself with a series of experts and their accompanying instruments: Holloway Roberts, accompanied by Wax Hook and Jed Leeder; Navidson, accompanied by Tom and Reston, as well as his camera and filmic skills; and Zampano, applying the ideas of real and spurious critical scholars.

The machinations of the house, however, go undiagnosed by the experts and their instruments: Roberts, Hook, Leeder, and Navidson himself (accompanied by his brother, Tom, and his professorial friend, Reston), despite their successful record of past explorations, are lost or nearly lost looking for an explanation. Nor can Zampano, Truant, and the decorated critical experts who parade their ideas past in the textual footnotes fully solve the mystery. In *House of Leaves*, hauntedness is postmodernist: it happens for no clear reason. In Mark Bailey's study, *American Nightmares*, one theme evident in other American haunted house tales seems to be conspicuously missing from Danielewski's: *the discovery of provenance for supernatural events*. Such provenance is often architecturally complicated. Buildings are haunted due to the violated boundaries of past histories—they may have been built, for instance, atop sacred sites or burial grounds. Buildings might also be subject to hauntedness because they secretly conceal the unburied. No such implication of provenance is ever revealed in *House of Leaves*. This genre-evocative novel also, then, moonlights as a dysfunctional detective novel whose mystery remains unsolved. Its violation of the formulaic, more traditional haunted house tale, and its neglect of historical narrative in other respects to the American novel, parallels the experimentalism of the avant-gardist, or of the urban planners of the past century, planners such as Baron Haussmann, who seemed more than willing to eradicate spaces of the past with their renovations.

Although Poe's tale never reveals the sinister illness which afflicts Madeline and Roderick Usher, Danielewski's novel ushers us into the modern age, diagnosing its occupants with phobias born into history as a consequence of modern warped space. These phobias help construct the novel's characters. Karen Green, for instance, suffers from a "crippling claustrophobia" at the first appearance of the mysterious hallway, and this phobia constructs her absence as a character. Narrative co-conspirators Johnny Truant and Zampano suffer from a case of agoraphobia whose growing potency parallels the growth of the house they unravel in their tales. At various junctures in the novel, Truant intimates that he and Zampano are housebound due to the pathological spell the inner narrative the novel has conjured and placed upon their respective psyches. Vertiginous phobias of the void, or *horror vacui*, like the perturbation of Poe's narrator as he gazes into the tarn, or the ill after effects Anthony Vidler describes with respect to Pascal's carriage accident(an experience which led to an inability to go out in the world, as well as later postulations of "infinity inscribed within the infinite," gradually paralyzes Navidson's brother, whose alcoholism worsens. Tom hesitates to enter the basement, and for much of the story, must occupy a chair at the top of the stairs.

In addition, *House of Leaves* exemplifies Anthony Vidler's contention that modernist space warps as a consequence of the simultaneous intersection of several media. The novel conflates varied forms of media: it is a gothic horror novel/artist's *book* about a *film* made by a *photographer*. The concept of space is hence bent through several different frames of media in the novel. Space is further complicated by Danielewski's experimentalist twists and exploitations of the book as artistic medium. The word "house" is distinguished from the rest, repeatedly appearing as the sole word represented in the color blue, inviting readers to consider its otherness. Index and appendices offer windows into the text. Differing typographies present the testimonies of Zampano, Truant, and critical scholars, and indicate varied levels of authority. Johnny Truant's text, for instance, appears in Courier, the print of the common typewriter, whereas the editor's comments appear in Bookman—a more authoritative type. As Martin Brick has noted, "footnotes invade the main body of the text, creating windows and rooms that lead the reader to turn and tunnel through the book"(Brick 8). The text isolates one or a few words on the page and invites interpretations of blank space. It disorients its reader, redirecting words in sideways patterns, and even turns words upside down for entire pages. The spatial notions the novel represents bend into even greater dimensions due to its narrative construct; the book offers its readers no less than three narrators. As some critics have mentioned, this multidimensional magic trick mimics the floorplan and verticality of an actual three-story house. The novel doubles as a film narrated and critically explicated by an enigmatic blind man, Zampano. Narrative space is warped still further: we "discover" the house and its story as a found text, through the digressions and meandering ideas of an unreliable narrator, professional ne'er-do-well, tattoo artist and amateur editor, Johnny Truant.

Multiplicity, often a troubling characteristic of the modern city, forms another disquieting facet of Danielewski's postmodern suburban nightmare. City residents customarily move to the country to simplify their lives, to avoid traffic and overcrowded urban conditions. Early twentieth century sociologists like Georg Simmel posited the detrimental side effects of urbanity, which included isolation and dehumanization. In his essay "The Metropolis and Mental Life," Simmel wrote that "the same fundamental motive was at work, namely the resistance of the individual to being leveled, swallowed up in the social-technological mechanism." The modern urban citizen, perhaps now as much as ever, fears an incomprehensible city of multiplicity, one which will deliver and abandon him to the wrong part of town at the wrong time. Somewhere in the psyche lurks the fear that the city may multiply beyond understandable blueprint and map, beyond human comprehension. Such a city will present too many stimuli, as well as symbology and dimensions beyond his control. *House of Leaves*, in part present due to confluence of narration—Navidson, Zampano, Johnny Truant, and the critical perspectives constantly lodged in the extensive teams of footnotes—leave the reader, as well as Navidson's family and friends, stranded, lost in Borgesian labyrinths of house, and the sprawling multiplicity of a city of many texts within one.

The problem posed in *House of Leaves* appears to have occurred to Italo Calvino when he wrote in "Cybernetics and Ghosts," "the more enlightened our houses are, the more their walls ooze with ghosts. Dreams of progress and reason are haunted by nightmares." Danielewski may have made modern renovations to the traditional haunted house, renovations complicated by modernist progress since Poe, but that house remains recognizably American, in part due to its suspicious treatment of experts, and to the self-directed target of its social critique. This house astonishes us with modern American absence and indifference, and with our homelessness within our own homes, with what Will Slocumbe calls "the absence *of* the house *within* the house"(2). It haunts us with how little progress we've made, with the poverty overflowing from our cities, and with the hollow foundation of American values, a hollowness which, like the house, threatens to swallow America whole. The house on Ash Tree Lane haunts us with excess and greed, with its accurate critique of the materialistic, empty American dream. Perhaps warped spaces in *House of Leaves* might be best understood as the rippling premonition of air and idea trying to form a dystopia, a terrible, barren, apocalyptic city that might one day take shape. They may just be a shudder or a modern tremor remaining from that most unstable proprietor of dreams, Roderick Usher, when he gazed into space, and confessed so many years ago, "I dread the events of the future..." Nonetheless, however, *House of Leaves*, with its experimentalism, ingenuity, and erudition, haunts us also with the possibility of how frighteningly fine a space the pages of the American novel might be.

Works Cited

Abel, Darrel. "A Key to the House of Usher." in *Interpretations of American Literature,* edited by Charles Feidelson, Jr., and Paul Brodtkorb, Jr., Oxford University Press, 1959, pp. 51-62.Print.

Bachelard, Gaston. *The Poetics of Space.* New York: The Orion Press, 1964. Print.

Bailey, Mark. *American Nightmares: The Haunted House Formula in American Popular Fiction.* Bowling Green, Ohio: Bowling Green State University Popular Press, 1999. Print.

Berman, Marshall. *All that is Solid Melts into Air.* Boston: Penguin, 1982. Print.

Brick, Martin. *Palimpsest Address: Time, Space, Memory, and the Unstable Architecture of Mark Z. Danielewski's House of Leaves.* MA Thesis. University of Wisconsin-Oshkosh, Oshkosh, Wisconsin, 2003. Print.

Castle, Terry. *The Female Thermometer: 18th Century Culture and the Invention of the Uncanny.* New York: Oxford University Press, 1995. Print.

Pahl, Dennis. *Architects of the Abyss.* Columbia, MO: University of Missouri Press, 1989. Print.

Danielewski, Mark. *House of Leaves.* New York: Pantheon, 2000. Print.

Freud, Sigmund. "The Uncanny." 10 May 2010. Web.
<<http://wwwrohan.sdsu.edu/~amtower/uncanny.html>>

Fusco, Richard. *Maupassant and the American Short Story: The Influence of Form at the Turn of the Century.* State College, PA: Pennsylvania State University Press, 1994. Print.

Hall, Peter. *Cities of Tomorrow.* Malden, MA: Blackwell Publishing, 1988. Print.

Murphy, Bernice M. *The Suburban Gothic in American Popular Culture.* New York: Palgrave MacMillan, 2009. Print.

Poe, Edgar Allan. "The Fall of the House of Usher." *Great Short Works of Edgar Allan Poe.* New York: Harper and Row, 1970. Print.

Slocumbe, Will. "This is Not for You": Nihilism and the House that Jacques Built. Modern Fiction Studies 51.1 (2005) 88-109. Print.

Vidler, Anthony. *The Architectural Uncanny: Essays in the Modern Unhomely.* Cambridge, MA: MIT Press, 1992. Print.

Vidler, Anthony. *Warped Space.* Cambridge, MA: MIT Press, 2001. Print.

Wilbur, Richard. "The House of Poe." *Modern Critical Views: Edgar Allan Poe.* Ed. Harold Bloom. New York: Chelsea House Publishers, 1985.

Daniel Grandbois
3 Conversation Pieces
from the forthcoming *Unlucky Lucky Tales*

Body

*Ben Marcus's "The Age of Wire and String" in Conversation
with Francis Ponge's "Taking the Side of Things"*

Tossed on a trash pile in an awkward pose. Swelling of hands, feet, and eyes renders them uninhabitable.

A mother cleans a child's mouth with a finger. "One must construct a usable garment from the four things: soil, straw, bark, and water."

Extremely thin skin is cooked onto their bodies, which begin to whistle from minor holes in the heat.

The stripping is easily done. The body is wrapped in cloth and then corrected with water and straw. Everything recovers its form.

The wires that generate sadness are attached. The effects will not be felt till spring. When the muscles fill like sponges, when the buds sprout again, they will know what is going on.

Milk

Vladmimir Voinovich's "Private Ivan Chonkin" in Conversations with Alexander Vvedensky's "Christmas at the Ivanovs"

The suckling turned out wrong. She took care of him anyway, put hot water bottles on his belly, wrapped him up in her kerchief.

How did it happen? A black crow flew over her, and a white devil with no arms or legs gave him red ears and made them stick out, made him fat-bellied and hairy. And now the clock keeps running like the milk from her breasts.

At the other end of the village, cattle are lowing. She spits on her hands and sets back to work. She is capable of doing anything. Here is her son. He swings around her like a pendulum, and the Milky Way swings around them both.

The Gate

Magdalena Tulli's "Dreams and Stones" in Conversation with Daniel Grandbois' "Unlucky Lucky People"

Fate had presented him with tasks that were petty and inconsequential. How many spadefuls of earth had to be dug? While he worked, they moved around him slowly like sick people. The days were counted and planned out many years in advance.

All he had to go on were the pieces of toast left at his feet. He ate the toasts, pondering his fate.

Wandering further than he'd meant to, he found a little pine grown out of a rock. It was, he imagined, a gate. The muscles in his face intimated the existence of a bright stalk of matter in him that wanted out.

"When it's done, it's done," he murmured. Only then will it be possible to distinguish day from night.

They presented their demands in raised voices, sometimes stopping and staring. How startled they would be when he loomed unexpectedly out of the whiteness.

He turned the knob and swung open the gate.

 # RICHARD CROW

DO THE CROWS...

Do the crows build nests? They build them from your lost toys.

Do the crows feed? They feed upon your missing keys.

Do the crows speak? They speak only if you cut them.

Do the crows steal? No, they take your eyes and leave you coins.

 Nisi Shawl
Just Between Us

Dolores opened the closet door. Here was the problem. A dead woman hung by her neck, suspended from the cross bar by a man's tie. Violet in color, probably silk from the look of the knot. She shut the door quickly and called up her landlady. This early that meant turning on the TV that Little Girl used to watch cartoons.

Mrs. Pawkes was dressed for golf. Her clothing glowed a golden green in on the oblong screen. Her sharp-chinned, line-seamed face managed to project warm but distracted concern as she assured Dolores that the dead women were nothing to worry about.

"'Women?' You mean this isn't the only one?"

"Well, I've had to take care of one a week now for—seems like maybe the last couple of months. But it's just like the refugees, isn't it?"

"No, Mrs. Pawkes, it is not." The last time she came in, Dolores had opened the closet door to find a huddled group of thin, brown, anxious people, clutching fearfully at blankets, newspapers, cooking pots. The detritus of displacement. "Corpses smell. Worse," she amended. "And I had to come back before I wanted to. I think they scared Little Girl. She's gone out."

"Oh, I'm so sorry. The poor thing." The image of Mrs. Pawkes switched from head-and-shoulders to full length as she removed her bag of clubs and leaned it against something—a wall or a doorway, it wasn't quite clear. Dolores kept a shallow focus. "I wish I'd known. She didn't say anything...."

"Well, what did you expect?" Little Girl was barely verbal. She must be aware of Mrs. Pawkes from the landlady's brief visits to the apartment. But otherwise there was very little contact between the two. They certainly didn't talk.

"I just didn't have anywhere else to put them, Dolores, but down there. They keep—popping up. I wish I could tell you where from."

"I'll look into it. Meanwhile, what am I supposed to do about Little Girl?"

"Send someone after her, I guess...unless you'd rather go yourself?"

"You know there isn't room enough for both of us out there."

"Well, I'm sure you'll think of something, dear. You're so resourceful." Mrs. Pawkes glanced longingly over her shoulder at her golf clubs. The vision began to fade. Dolores closed her eyes. She could have held it together, maintained transmission, but what would be the point? As usual, everything was up to her.

She opened her eyes, massaging the wrinkles where her eyebrows furrowed together. She looked around the place. Not bad, except for the smell. She was in the upper story of a white-painted frame house. Old. Interesting. Lots of windows with tiny panes shaped like diamonds, crescents, tears. Hardwood floors, oriental rugs. Little Girl had left her playthings strewn around the apartment: a rocking horse, cardboard boxes painted to look like bricks. A pink tutu and a cone-shaped hat, white-spangled chiffon streaming from its peak. On the enamel-topped kitchen table a bubble pipe and a tub full of sudsy water waited next to a bowl of soggy cereal.

How could Mrs. Pawkes have been so insensitive? This was supposed to be a safe place. Not a morgue. And Little Girl wasn't really equipped to handle most of what went on outside. How to get her back?

She sat down to think on a love-seat that hadn't been there when she came in. It was hers. She recognized the blue wool upholstery from her last time in. The longer she stayed, the more the place would bear her mark.

Send someone after her. Sure, but who? Dolores and Little Girl were the main tenants, the oldest and biggest ones. There were others, though. Neighbors. Guests. Dolores struggled to classify those she knew.

Patcheddy. She was like Little Girl, only thin and weak and poor. That big, red, roaring—Dolores had never given that a name. Call it Red. Red was too scary to help with this. And Patcheddy wasn't much good for anything, except to whine. It had to be someone small enough so they could both fit outside, but strong enough to bring Little Girl back in.

There was a tapping at one of the windows. A big black bird with blue and white wings was pecking at the glass. Dolores got up to let it in, then hesitated with the window open only a crack. "Who is it?"

It was Hermie.

"Oh, yes." Little Girl's imaginary playmate. She swung the casement wide and he flew in. Hermie had come to Little Girl along with the mumps and an interminable stay in bed. Usually, though, he looked more like light reflecting from a glass of water—or nothing at all. "What brings you here? And why so—so—"

So visible. The bird cocked his head knowingly. He was practicing. He wanted to go outside, to find Little Girl, and he needed to practice pretending to be real.

"Perfect!" she exclaimed. She sat back down on the love seat, and Hermie hopped onto the far arm. "Thank you, thank you, thank you."

Actually, the going out part would be easy. For him. Finding her, too. But he would need help bringing her back.

"But I'm too big to get outside while she's still there."

But she could help inside. She had to. She had to get rid of the dead women. She had to stop them coming. Otherwise he could find Little Girl, but what good would that do? She'd never come back in.

"Okay, Hermie. Okay. I'll see what I can do." He flew back to the windows. They were French, now, with crystal doorknobs. He flapped back and forth noisily while she walked over, turned a knob and pushed. There was a balcony on the other side, weeping black wrought iron. Hermie flew out over it and became one with the powder blue mist beyond.

Am I all right they keep asking, asking. I always tell them no. My favorite word. It's the best. Nonononono. I use it all the time.

I'm hungry. I want a candy bar, or an ice cream. I ask the waiter for one I remember that is orange. A Dreamsicle is the name. But when it comes it is all melted in a glass. No stick. And it tastes like medicine. Nasty. I drink it anyway.

I try again. A Heath Bar, too, is all melted. Everything in this place is nasty and served in a cup. I'm going to leave. It's closing anyway. They want to know if I need them to call me a cab. I use my word and go.

It's pretty out in the dark. There aren't too many things to see. The wind kisses me with long, dry kisses, brushing down my cheeks. I think the wind is like a pretty young lady aunt. She runs around doing interesting things, so she doesn't have to tell you how big you're getting. And she kisses you, but then she moves away, not holds you tight so you can't go and it's scary and your word won't even work.

There is a park, but I'm not supposed to go in there. Bad men are waiting to hurt a Little Girl. But if they saw me they would think I was big, like Dolores is. Only still they might want to hurt me. Anyways, I don't have to want to go there, because out of the park flies a bird I like. Dark and dry and friendly, the way the wind is in this night. I hold out my finger and he grabs it with his feet. It hurts, but not too much, and also it feels good. The bird's feet are

strong. *It is holding on to me and I am holding it up.*
Come on, says the bird. Let's go.

Dolores cut the woman down. She stunk, like old rotten stew. Her face was blotched and flaccid. She collapsed in an ugly heap on the closet floor.

Dolores thought that was strange. Shouldn't you be stiff if you were dead long enough to smell? But it made the woman a lot easier to handle. All she had to figure out now was what to do with her.

She took her in the bathroom. While hot water ran into the big white tub she removed the woman's clothing. It was basically nondescript: grey sweater, beige and grey and cream plaid skirt. Underwear from Penney's, with comfortable, band-sewn legs. Little balls of rolled-up lint on the bra. Support pantyhose. Loafers.

Everything from the waist down was soiled. What wasn't smelled like spoiled meat from long, close contact with the corpse. She sat the body on the edge of the tub and guided it gently into the water. It slid so the head was under. She didn't see how that could matter.

While the corpse was soaking she rinsed out the skirt and things in the toilet bowl, thinking how she was going to do this seven more times, if she could find the rest. It was worse than having kids. With them you could use disposables.

She rinsed the dirty clothes out again in the sink, then had to go down to the laundry room to get a basket. She didn't like the basement. It never seemed very clean. Too many things were the same there as outside.

The furnace had long twisting ducts coming out of it, like fat metallic tentacles. Over in the far corner there was a freezer. Nobody used it anymore, not since her mother disappeared. It was chained shut and locked.

When she came back upstairs the body was gone. The water in the tub was clean. She pulled out the stopper by its chain, took the clothes down and loaded them in the machine. Delicate fabrics, short cycle. She left the machine whirring and sloshing away, went to the kitchen and made herself a cup of tea. Then she called up Mrs. Pawkes again, to see if she had any possible clue as to what the hell was going on.

Now Dolores had been inside a while she could picture her landlady on any flat surface. The side of the toaster worked.

"Well, dear," said Mrs. Pawkes, "I really don't know where I put them all." She raised a be-ringed finger in protest of Dolores' anger. "In my defense—don't frown, you'll make lines, you don't want to end up looking like me, do you?—In my defense I have to say it's mostly because you two *change* the place around so *much*. I mean, I'm sure I could find them, but they're probably not where I put them because where I put them is undoubtedly *gone*, you see...." She waited for Dolores to do or say something to show she understood. Dolores nodded tiredly.

"And as far as where they're coming from, Dolores, I really couldn't say."

"You don't have even the slightest idea?"

"Well, it's not the sort of thing...." She trailed off again. "It's a delicate subject, I'm afraid. I don't think your father would approve." Dolores thought maybe she should just give up. There were subjects Mrs. Pawkes refused to talk about at all. Sex. Bodily functions. Violence of any sort. The fight two months back, right before her mother had run off—Mrs. Pawkes referred to it as, "That discussion between your parents." Sometimes Dolores wondered how she ever wound up being their landlady. That was likely the secret, though. Being so above it all.

"Thanks," she said, hoping she didn't sound too sarcastic. "I'll let you know how it all works out."

His name is Hermie. I know him. I like him, but I don't want to go back. I say no.

He says o.k., but it's going to get cold later. Maybe we can find a donut shop. We do. It has a roof like an orange skirt swirling out dancing. The walls are all glass. I wonder if they'll let me in carrying a crow.

Magpie, says Hermie. I am a magpie, not a crow. Anyway, they probably won't even see me.

Why? I ask. I open the door. Hermie is on my shoulder now.

Because I'm a figment of your imagination.

Oh, I say. I thought you were a magpie. It's a joke. I know you can be more than one thing at a time.

Quiet, says Hermie. You don't want them to think you're crazy, do you?

There were dead women all over, once she started looking. Stuffed under the kitchen sink. In the laundry hamper. The pantry. One was wedged in the little space between the fridge and the wall. One was in the spare room, neatly tucked in bed. She had to wash the sheets and mattress pad as well when she did that one's clothes.

They all dissolved in the tub. Their clothes stayed. She had a whole wardrobe of shapeless, baggy, colorless garments on hangers in the laundry room. No two outfits were identical, but they might as well have been. Mix-and-match.

All except the things this one wore. The one she held in her hands. This corpse was only eight or nine inches tall. It still smelled awful. She had found it in the sugar bin.

Washing them got rid of the dead women, but it didn't bring her any closer to the problem's cause. This one was obviously special. Maybe if she did something different this time she could revive it enough to ask it some questions. She thought.

The cookie sheets were in a tall, narrow cupboard made just for them. She rinsed off the heaviest, the best one, while waiting for the oven to pre-heat. Stuck it in for a moment to dry. Took it out and coated it with butter, deciding against a dusting of flour on top of that.

She removed the doll-like clothes and sponged off the small, naked corpse, nervously expecting it to dissolve and disappear. It didn't. She laid the body on the cookie sheet and brushed it with lemon juice. What else? She got some raisins, put two over the dead woman's eyes, one between her slack lips. Was that it? Almost. With a paring knife she cut another raisin in two, then stuck the resulting halves over the nipples. That looked right. The oven was ready. She slid the woman in, set the timer, and put everything away.

I get two fried cakes and a jelly donut. And hot chocolate. It's really good. I hand up crumbs to Hermie where he's still sitting on my shoulder. I giggle and wonder if everybody else just sees pieces of donut disappear into the air. Or maybe they are floating inside Hermie's invisible, imaginary crow-belly.

Magpie, he says, and I laugh out loud.

Am I all right? No.

Nothin' says lovin' like somethin' from the oven. Dolores didn't really need the timer to know when the dead woman was done. The aroma said it all. She smelled kind of good, actually. Kind of—juicy. Delicious, really. Like baked apples. The odor spoke to Dolores invitingly as she pulled out the cookie sheet. She spatulaed up the corpse and transferred it to a cooling rack. Now she'd get some answers.

The dead woman, however, was obstinately silent.

All right, thought Dolores. She reached out and broke off an arm. It tasted sweet and gingery. She closed her eyes to analyze the flavor. Sugar and spice and everything nice. She opened them and saw the pan was empty.

The dead woman must have shinnied down a table leg. She was running across the kitchen floor, headed for the basement steps.

"Oh, no," said Dolores. "Don't go down there." She hurried but she was too late. The little woman fell headlong down the stairs and broke into pieces at the bottom.

Dolores walked down to her carefully, holding on to the rail. Why was she so sad? The other corpses were gone, too, but she'd never cared one way or another about them. She started crying. She picked up the pieces, brushed off some bits of lint. She took a bite of one big fragment; she thought maybe it was the head. In the far corner the padlocked freezer clicked and hummed to life. Then she remembered.

Two policemen come in. I don't know if I like that. But they just sit down at the other counter, which is this really ugly color like moldy bread. That's why me and Hermie picked the pretty bright orange one on this side.

The man brings them coffee and long, twisty rolls before they even ask for anything. Then he comes back to me again. And I tell him no. No and no and no and no and no. I keep saying no, even after he walks away. Maybe he will get it.

He goes and bothers the police instead. They are talking real quiet and I can't hear the words, but Hermie says uh-oh. I shut up.

One of the police gets off his stool and comes over to me. He calls me ma'am. Do I need help?

I think I better go. It's time to be inside.

Dolores came out. Dolores answered. She said yes. She could use some help. Dolores said there was a problem at her house. She said the policemen should come with her and see. It had to do with the way her mother disappeared a couple of months ago, and how her father had acted ever since. She gave them her name and address, and said she'd be glad to accept their offer of a lift. Yes, it was kind of dangerous being out alone this late.

She wanted to know if they had anything in the squad car that would be good at breaking chains or busting a lock. If not, maybe they ought to stop by the station on the way. She assured them that would be okay. What she wanted to show them was in the freezer. It wasn't going anywhere. It would be all right.

I'm glad Hermie brought me back inside. The policemen were scaring me, and it's good to be home again. He says there won't be anymore ghosts to come, either. Dolores made it better.
Dolores is nice. But she always puts away all my toys, and then I have a hard time finding them again. What's left now is my goldfish. I sit down and watch them swimming around and around and around. I wonder if they think they're going anywhere, or if they know what they are in.

Richard Schindler
Featured Artist Gallery & Interview

02

03

04

05

06

07

08

09

10

11

DRAWN TO BLACK AND WHITE: THE ILLUSTRATIVE ART OF RICHARD SCHINDLER

Interviewed by Michael Chocholak

Richard A. Schindler is an Associate Professor of Art at Allegheny College. He has a B.A. from Gettysburg College, an M.A. from UMass-Amherst, and a Ph.D. in art history from Brown University. His area of specialty is 19th-century European art, most notably the study of Victorian painting and illustration with side trips into the alleyways of French Symbolism and Art Nouveau.

Illustrations in black and white have always been my favorite form of art. The great illustrators from the turn of the last century, such maestros as Aubrey Beardsley, Willy Pogany, Harry Clarke, Howard Pyle, and William Heath Robinson, decorated the halls of my imagination from my earliest days as an avid reader. I also grew up with the art of Jack Kirby, Steve Ditko, Frank Frazetta, Jeffrey Jones, Michael Kaluta, and Barry Windsor-Smith, all masterful practitioners of the graphic art. In my own humble way I have followed their path, illustrating books and magazines dealing with themes of fantasy and science fiction. My artistic aspirations are in some ways a counter-balance to the sometimes stodgy professional parameters of my work as an art historian. I love to explore the ways in which mass, or "low" culture intersect with and inhabit the confines of fine, or "high" art and vice-versa.

MEZ: *Most of us draw to some extent throughout our lives, but few of us would consider ourselves as having any distinction as a graphic artist... when did you realize this would be your focus, your path?*

RAS: I'd like to say that I had some kind of epiphany along the way, but that wasn't really the case with drawing. I got interested in drawing seriously during high school, although I had been a doodler from way back. I wanted to be the next Jack Kirby, because I had discovered his art for Marvel Comics when I was twelve or thirteen years old. *That* was an epiphany, reading the Fantastic Four, Thor, the X-Men, the Avengers, Captain America, et al. My desire was to emulate Kirby's style; I even did a comic book in my senior year about a character with the ability to use carbon in some sort of superhero fashion. I don't remember much about that comic now, but my English teacher at the time was very supportive. She had my friends and me do a reading of the comic in front of the class. That may have been the reinforcement that I needed, since I took no art classes in high school (not part of the college track, unfortunately).

I took art classes in college, but my main interest became art history. One of the best classes that I took, though, was a drawing class with an adjunct professor (filling in for a professor on sabbatical leave). He was the one who suggested that I should take an art history class—"You like history and you like art, why not take art history?"—I like to tell my students that at that moment the heavens opened up, a beatific light streamed down, and an angelic choir began to sing. It was certainly a deciding moment in my search for a potential career. The history of modern art was one of the first classes that I took. The teacher started with the Pre-Raphaelites and the art was so stunningly beautiful to me that I knew what I wanted to do with my life after that moment. That interest in the Victorian era was reinforced by the work that Barry Windsor Smith did for the Conan comics and the prints he did afterwards. BWS melded the historical style with his illustrative art in a powerful way.

It's with thanks to Mark and Michael Ziesing (proprietors of the now-defunct Ziesing Book Emporium in Willimantic, CT) that I really felt like an illustrator, working on posters, bookmarks, and several short stories. Two things stick out in my mind from that period: doing the chapter vignettes for Mark's independent publication of Gene Wolfe's *Free, Live Free* (1984) and the cover illustrations for *Instead of @ Magazine*, an anarchist publication put out by Michael's Lysander Spooner Society. I also owe a debt of gratitude to Michael G. Adkisson and *New Pathways* magazine for the chance to illustrate a number of stories and one cover illustration. And then, of course, David Memmott asked me to do some illustrations for *Ice River* and some Wordcraft publications. I especially liked the assignments that involved the illustration of fantasist short stories, especially those of Conger Beasley, Jr. He had an imagination that sparked some of my favorite illustrations; his prose pushed me to really think beyond the use of obvious imagery.

All of these opportunities made me feel like a full-fledged illustrator, a sporadic feeling I must admit. My career as an illustrator has never been one of constancy in terms of drawing every day and developing recognition outside of a very small body of readers and viewers. Every illustrator that I love worked without cease on their art, driven to work, always developing, never satisfied with half-measures. I have let myself be distracted by life in ways that seem to interfere in that kind of obsessive focus that great (and even not-so-great) artists bring to bear on their life and work. Of course, the brutal selfishness that attends that kind of obsession has been well documented in numerous artistic biographies. Many people do not really think about how dedicated you need to be to make it as an artist (in all meanings of the term). Self-motivation is key and a willingness to realize that the world at large does not have any obligation to recognize or embrace your art because your heart is pure and your intentions honorable.

MEZ: Angels and portraits of musicians— why these? Why not, say, famous magicians or heroes of the Crimean War?

RAS: Hmmm. Heroes of the Crimean War, now that's an idea… I have always been fascinated by angels (and demons, too, just for the record). Lots of angels populate the art of the Victorians (Dante Gabriel Rossetti, George Frederick Watts, Frederick, Lord Leighton, Edward Burne-Jones, Simeon Solomon, Evelyn Pickering, and Eleanor Fortescue Brickdale) and American illustrators of the 19th century (Howard Pyle and N.C. Wyeth, for example). Throw the Art Nouveau era and European Symbolist art into the mix and the air is aflutter with angelic wings. I started doing my own Christmas cards about 25 years ago and angels seemed like an appropriate subject for those cards as the years passed.

Another source for my angel cards comes from the Italian and Northern European Renaissance, angel musicians in particular. I've always liked early music of the medieval and Renaissance periods, as well as the musical instruments. My latest series of images relates to that interest, with angels playing the serpent, the viola da gamba, and the lute. I have also done some angels based on Persian and Turkish models; I've always had a soft spot for Islamic art of the 16th and 17th century.

The portraits of musicians I particularly like came about because I'm getting older and so are they. I wanted to show Bob Dylan, Neil Young, Leonard Cohen, Joni Mitchell, and Johnny Cash as people who have seen and suffered a great deal. The kind of music they make has changed with their aging, so why not show them expressing the kind of fraught, powerful emotions that their music contains? It's hard for me to measure how much these singer/songwriters influenced my life, yet they certainly made living a deeper, more spiritual experience for me.

12   13

MEZ: Your angels and pagan spirits have a very human quality to them... engaging, not aloof, ethereal, or detached. Your musicians appear haunted by the pain of their passion... as if they've had a glimpse beyond the veil. Is there a connection between these portrayals?

RAS: Well, I hope my angels are just a bit ethereal. They are otherworldly beings, after all. I do like the idea of humanizing the divine, since angels are considered holy messengers and intermediaries between God and humanity. The images are relatively simple in that I concentrated on the details of a figure, usually holding some kind of object, standing against a blank background. The focus is held to the details of the garments, the shape and patterning of the wings, the facial expression, and the suggested symbolism of the object or instrument, for examples, the candle for faith, a book for knowledge or wisdom, a rose for passion and suffering. If people see some kind of emotional resonance without noticing the symbolism, that's fine with me. I drew the angels in pen and ink, because I wanted a strong image that could be easily reproduced. I like working with pen and ink, especially Mars Staedtler technical pens, to get a crisply flowing line that works so well for drapery, feathers, and hair.

The portraits were done in pencil and, occasionally, charcoal. The subtler gradations of tone convey more effectively the kind of introspective pathos that I wish to capture. I see faces as a kind of emotive topography; every seam and fissure tells a story. The glossiness of graphite also works well for the luminosity of the eyes and the sheen of hair. The point is to get the viewer to feel like they are looking into the "soul" of the portrayed person. I've always liked to play with the frames as well, so that the image breaks the boundaries here and there. The effect pushes the image to the very foreground and, one hopes, directly engages the viewer with the mutely appealing glance of the protagonist.

MEZ: I would assume from your portraits that music plays an important role in your life. Do you listen to music when you work on your art? If so, what kind & do you use it as a background or do you draw from it more directly for your work?

RAS: I like to listen to music before I do art work; most of the music I really like would be a siren's call that would distract from my attention as I tried to draw. I suppose that there is music that can serve as a background to visual creation, but even good, solid instrumental music tends to wend its merry way into my audial synapses in ways that deflect me from the task at hand. I suppose certain musical practitioners invented the concepts of easy listening (or "musical wallpaper," as one critic defined it) in order to create a kind of music that does not intrude on your conscious mind or placates the listener with a comfortable sonic blanket. When people talk about the "soundtrack of your life" I inwardly wince for the fact that anyone who considers music to be a backdrop for daily life has not really listened to real music. Real music grabs you and shakes you up, alters your perception of the world as you listen, sticks in your mind even after you decided you didn't like it that first time you heard it, and doesn't brook any interference from other sensorial sources. You shouldn't multi-task when you're listening to great music.

My tastes are pretty eclectic when it comes to music, so I have a whole plethora of favorite musicians. Depending on the mood, I listen to anything from folk music to raw punk (especially the early stuff), jazz combos to medieval plainsong, trip hop to electronica.

I have an especial fondness for the music I grew up with, but I'm willing to listen to anything new that does not pander to popular tastes. Let's face it, individual taste in music is hard to pin down in terms of some kind of impartial ideal of quality; one does not have to be a trained listener, though, to know there's a sharp difference in abilities and imagination that separate, say, the jazz of Miles Davis from that of Kenny G. If the latter was playing in the background as I worked on a drawing, I doubt that the music would impinge itself on my consciousness.

The biggest impact that music has on me is in the power and imagery of the lyrics. I've always been impressed by the Dylan songs that use apparently simple phrasing with an inspired cadence and rhythm to propel those lyrics into the listener's mind. A song like "Not Dark Yet" already starts at a level of sullen enervation and then builds to a bone-deep despair that is engulfed in a "soup" of ringing guitar chords. My thoughts as I listen to the song circle around how I can make this into a sequential narrative that evokes the same visceral response as the music.

MEZ: *On the one hand, your lines are in stark contrast to the free space, yet once inside those lines the look is sumptuous, at times almost tactile. Why pen & ink?*

I work in pen and ink, because I was blown away by the work of Aubrey Beardsley when I was a young pup. Even to this day a Beardsley drawing fills me with an ineffable pleasure; each piece is so well crafted in its use of line, shape, pattern, and design. I've always been a fan of the graphic arts in terms of personal taste (it's somewhat different when it comes to professional interests). I seek to do the same things that Beardsley did in my drawings, although on my own terms. My instincts are caught between the flat abstraction of line and the 3D effects of hatching and cross-hatching. I also like to create a strong contrast between rich areas of black and stark white, with areas of elaborate detail moving throughout the image. My taste runs more toward the variety of realisms that one can find in 19th and 20th-century art and illustration, from Victorian narrative art to the renaissance of fantasy illustration in the 1960s. I'd like to think I was an artist who melds the realistic with the fantastic in intriguing ways like the artists I most appreciate.

When I illustrate a text I have two concerns: the illustration should do just that, illustrate, and the image should be striking enough to attract the reader's attention without deflecting from the importance of the text. When I did the cover illustration for Dave Memmott's poetry collection *Within the Walls of Jericho* I wanted to create an image that both reflected the title and worked like a conflation of poetic images. The impetus for the rock egg and the fortress walls came from René Magritte's famous painting *Castle in the Pyrenees* (1959). Since the egg shape suggested birth to me I drew a desert hawk emerging from a crack in the surface. Thus, the image suggested the durable, yet fragile rock pierced by the birth of something wild and fierce. I liken that birth to that of the artistic creation, whether it be a poem or a drawing.

Although drawings and prints have become accepted as aesthetic staples in the realm of the art world, most people still see a drawing as a first step toward a finished art work, culminating in a painting or a sculpture. Yet the illustration of books and magazines, the evolution of the comic strip and the editorial cartoon, and the emergence of the graphic novel from comic books argue for an alternative history of modernism that has its own protagonists and heroic moments. For instance, think of the contributions of Winsor McCay, George Herriman, Milt Caniff, Alex Raymond, Charles Schulz, and Bill Watterston to the humble comic strip, an art form that was already pretty sophisticated from the get-go. The dichotomy of high art/low art only works to a certain degree; the interchange between so-called "fine" art and the art of mass culture (what Clement Greenberg would indiscriminately call "kitsch") is so much more intricate and complex than the mavens of high modernism would admit.

MEZ: Does creating art draw you into the world or bring you out of it? Who and what are your influences and why? Whose art do you enjoy and why?

RAS: To be of the world is to be in the world, biblically speaking. I suppose I could say that my fantasy art takes me out of the world, while my political art draws me into the world. However, in order for fantasy art to be effective there must be some element of recognizable imagery or symbolism that serves to give the viewer access to that fantastic realm. By that same reasoning one could say that there needs to be something unrecognizable in strong political art that helps the viewer to understand the usual message in an unusual and insightful way. Good fantasy art invites you to spend some time with the visual narrative, evoking surprise or suggesting an alternative reading of the natural world. Good political art needs to be understood quickly by the audience or, like a badly told joke, no one gets it.

I've already mentioned quite a few influences on my art and my artistic sensibility. One of the major influences on my tender teenage psyche was Frank Frazetta; the first Conan cover literally stopped me in my tracks as I perused the book rack in the local pharmacy. The publication of *The Studio* in the late 70s brought together a stellar group of my favorite artists: Barry Windsor-Smith, Jeff Jones, Michael W. Kaluta, and Bernie Wrightson; my deep affection for their art has continued to this day. My favorite comic book writers and artists are too numerous to mention, but I appreciate the fact that a small segment of the writing and picture-making in mainstream and independent comics have kept pace with my adult tastes and interests. I have been heartened by the rise of graphic novels that deal with serious themes and remarkable narratives, especially in the work of such stellar talents as Art Spiegelman, Alison Bechdel, Daniel Clowes, Charles Burns, Dave Mazzuchelli, and Chris Ware. Of especial note is Scott McCloud's *Understanding Comics*, the ur-text for anyone who takes sequential narrative seriously. I have to admit that my desire to write my own graphic novel is tempered by my inclination to write an academic study of graphic novels. Perhaps I can merge the two desires into one.

MEZ: Many graphic artists have a web page and show their work on the web, but beyond that there seems to be a major schism as far as using digital medium to create their art. How does your approach to & philosophy of art relate to the digital world and technology?

RAS: I think that the internet is a great place to exhibit art, and I created a website (rareavis.net) to exhibit some of my bookplates and angel images. This interview has reminded me that I should get my act together and add more images. Facebook with its photo caches is another place to display one's art. The limitation for someone of my advanced years, though, is to keep these sites updated. While providing access to such an array of information and services, the internet is also a time-sucking beast without peer.

Since I teach art history to young studio majors I see a lot of experimentation with digital media. I also see the application of digital effects of color and design to the use of traditional drawing techniques. Yet, no matter how conversant the student may be with software programs and digital illustration, one has to know how to handle composition, design, and materials if one wants to be a credible and credited artist. I have one current student interested in comic book art who starts with a conventional sketch and transfers the image to a design pad where she can use a stylus to capture the image in outline and then enhance this image with a broad ranging palette of colors. Her work benefits from her grasp of expressive painterly effects and dynamic action poses.

I will stay with more conventional drawing techniques, though, as I also retain my stubborn adherence to the handheld book. Nothing in the computer world has ever come close to duplicating the tactility of a handheld pen marking the surface of an eggshell-smooth paper with flowing ink line of a particularly opalescent black.

MEZ: *With the ever-growing web, instant, disposable everything and all-devouring pop culture, have you noticed a shift over the years in how your students relate to classical art?*

RAS: Popular culture sure does come in for some well deserved critical scourging, especially when the appeal is to the lowest common denominator of youth culture (think "Jersey Shore") or as a means to dispense virulent propaganda disguised as hard fact (think Rupert Murdoch and Fox News). Just because the technological world has superficially changed in sophistication and a questionable global culture seems nigh at hand does not mean that humanity itself has progressed to an equal level of moral, psychological, and emotional adulthood. For every great moment of thoughtful dialogue or inspired thinking there is an unraveling skein of vituperative commentary, outright mendacity, purposeful chicanery, and clot-minded ignorance. History becomes a story sold on the auction block by the loudest voices to the most gullible of audiences. Santayana's maxim that "Those who ignore history are condemned to repeat it" becomes even more sinister when history is not only ignored but invented out of whole cloth.

Certainly art and art history are not exempt from this clarion call to mediocrity. When *Newsweek* magazine chooses Jeff Koons and Damien Hirst as two out of ten of the most important artists of today the conclusion appears to be that embracing commercialism as the central subject matter of contemporary art is perfectly fine. If you're as self-confidently preening as Koons or as engagingly vapid as Hirst, the world is your oyster. Lest you think I'm some kind of cultural jihadist, I would like to say that there are plenty of contemporary artists who I admire and respect, from Mark Rothko and Francis Bacon to Kiki Smith and Takashi Murakami. As I remind my students there is art for almost any taste out there, you just have to look for it. Greater cultural savvy may lead to an even greater abundance of diverse art forms and astonishing new techniques.

However, a lack of familiarity with where contemporary art came from can have a debilitating effect on the variety and innovation of contemporary art. While today's students have access to a smorgasbord of images and information, that access does not guarantee some kind of implicit understanding of how to make good art. Also, there's no guarantee that young artists are going to want to make innovative art; the lure of craftsmanship sometimes becomes the be-all and end-all of the search for artistic success. The shopworn division between fine art (les beaux arts) and commercial art, though, does not hold water in today's marketplace. The best artists (and many are graphic designers and illustrators) have a refreshing grasp on how to use images of the past in inventive ways. I introduce my students to the multiple uses of past art, from the Renaissance to the modern and postmodern eras. No artist lives in a vacuum and the good ones attune themselves not only to their own time but to the gamut of styles that run from prehistoric times to the present. It's my job as an art historian to open up the realm of possibilities and to reinforce the need to study the past in order to make the best possible present.

MEZ: *What are your obsessions? What inspires you, infuriates you?*

I'm an obsessive reader, to the point of folly at times. I know that I have some quotidian task to be performed and I retreat into the literary world that I've lived in since I was five years old. I also collect art books, comic books, graphic novels, biographies, SF and fantasy novels and short stories, and social and cultural histories. My appetite for reading and collecting is voracious, to say the least. I also love noir (B movies with class), foreign, SF and fantasy films, and any film that takes the craft seriously. I watched "The Hangover" a while ago and wondered why people found this mean-spirited, morally vacuous movie to be, of all things, funny. On the other hand, films like "Winter's Bone" and the remake of "True Grit," just to name two favorites of the past year, reminded me of why I like film.

I would hope that my art, at its best, would tap into the same kind of emotional terrain, a willingness to look clearly at a broken world and come away with a gleam of hope and a spark of imagination.

No one was happier than I when comic book stories and characters began to show up as feature-length films, sometimes done with substance, wit, and grace. Unfortunately, the success of these films led to a deluge of comic book heroes and anti-heroes on the big screen. Coupled with Hollywood's adoration of CGI the experience in the theater became more an exercise in eye-candy and less one of respect for narrative and depth of character. Explosions supplant exposition, the blue screen becomes the chimerical backdrop to senseless action, and every element of story and symbolism is painstakingly parsed out for the audience as if no one ever had an original thought before they came to the theater. Now I'm torn between pleasure at the recognition that comic books and graphic novels are receiving and the nerd's desire to be left alone with my peculiar and personal interests. I'd certainly like to turn the fruits of that paradox into a graphic narrative of some kind.

Good teaching inspires me, not only to be the best teacher I can be but also to learn from my students. I applaud effective social action by young people to bring justice and equality to the disaffected, the disillusioned, the disenfranchised, and the marginalized. I certainly miss the opportunities I had early on in my life to make political art; it's not that easy when you've become a solid citizen within the academic system. I would love to contribute art work to anarchist publications again, although the collage seems to have been embraced to the exclusion of other artistic techniques by the political radicals. I like collage, just not enough to make them myself.

Too many things infuriate me. If someone had told me in the late '60s what the political and social landscape of America would look like in the 21st century, I would have been laughingly dismissive of such a dour outlook. What seemed then to be a hopeful sign that we were all growing up and changing the world for the better became a freethinker's nightmare. In fact the very notion of a freethinker has been co-opted by a motley group of conservative thugs, charlatans, snake oil merchants, provocateurs, and carnival barkers. They have systematically pillaged the economy, ravaged the environment, gutted the educational system, corrupted the moral principles of religious belief, stripped every individual's right to privacy, and made this country a playground for corporate hacks and wealthy sociopaths. It's my job to remind people that these problems did not just suddenly occur in recent times, these problems have been around for millennia. However, the crises that we all face now are that we are running out of time and too many Neros are fiddling as the world burns. At the same time, I can bring my curmudgeonly point of view into the classroom, but there's a limit to how far one can go in castigating "things as they are" and urging young people to embrace "things as they should be." In my art I don't have to observe the niceties of social behavior and I can do what I damn well please.

LIST OF PLATES

01 "Piranesian Spiral," pen & ink, 1991
02 "Daybreak 2," pen & ink, 2003
03 "Nightfall 2," pen & ink, 2003
04 "Yellowjacket," pen & ink, (cassette tape by Michael Chocholak), 1989
05 "Magic Deer," pen & ink, (cover art for Conger Beasley, Jr.), 1989
06 "The Sufferer," pen & ink, (illustration for W. Gregory Stewart), 2002
07 "The Blood of Dead Poets," pen & ink, (cover for Conger Beasley Jr.,), 1996
08 "Beauty and the Beast (Traditional version," pencil, 1992
09 "Beauty and the Beast (Punk version), pencil, 1992
10 "Odin—Tree of Wisdom," pen & ink, 2001
11 "Within the Walls of Jericho," pen & ink, (cover art for David Memmott), 1998
12 "Johnny Cash," pencil & charcoal, 2006
13 "Pensive Angel,"

Brian Evenson
The Jar

After Blau blegged for his hands for a year a guard removed him from the narrow cell and led him down a hall. The guard walked too quickly for Blau, who had not left the cell for more than a year. He tried to keep up, to move his curved and puss-ridden feet in rhythm to the guard's boots, not daring to speak even when he stumbled and fell. He caught most of the fall with the rough stumps of his arms, feeling the shock run up through his elbows.

The guard stooped, helped him up, and they continued a little slower.

"Thank you," said Blau.

The guard nodded.

"My name is Blau," said Blau.

"A pleasure," said the guard.

"Where are you taking me?"

"To your hands."

The hall they walked was intersected by other passages. Looking to the side as they crossed an intersection, Blau could see other intersections, the beginning of other halls, as far as he could see.

"Did you know my name already?" asked Blau, "before I told it to you?"

The guard struck him in the stomach hard but without heat. Blau fell and writhed on the floor a moment. Eventually the guard set him on his feet again.

"You are not allowed to speak," the guard said.

They walked forward in silence, the guard's heels ringing on the floor of the hall, Blau scuttling behind. He counted twelve intersections before the pain in his legs grew so great he could no longer keep count.

"I never knew your name," said the guard.

"What?"

"But I know your number."

"My number?"

"Your number," the guard said.

They walked on in silence. The guard was walking a little faster and Blau found himself hard-pressed to keep up.

"What is my number?"

The guard deftly removed a stick from his belt, struck Blau across the back. Blau cried out and tumbled forward. He lay on the ground, feeling the pain, felt himself being helped to his feet.

"You are not allowed to speak," said the guard.

They turned into a side hall, passed several steel doors. At the fourth or fifth door they stopped and the guard removed a ring of keys from his pocket. He tried a key in the lock, cursed, removed it. He began searching through the ring, holding each key close to his face, examining it. He put another key in the door. The door opened.

Taking Blau by the elbow, the guard pulled him in.

The room was perhaps fifty paces from end to end, a single huge light in the ceiling, a wheeled ladder standing beneath it. Covering the walls were shelves of jars. Blau counted them. From floor to ceiling were twenty-four tiers.

"Good luck," said the guard.

"What?" said Blau.

The guard gestured him forward. Blau approached a row of jars, staring into the nearest. He blocked out the glare on the glass with his forearm. The jar contained a thick liquid in which floated a preserved pair of hands. He looked at the next jar and found it too to contain a pair of hands, floating, palms open, fingers curled.

"They're hands," said Blau.

The guard twisted the keys in his hands. "That is what they are," he said.

"Whose are they?"

The guard shrugged, with one hand tucking in the back of his shirt.

"Which are mine?" asked Blau.

He watched the guard go out the door.

Blau turned and looked. Twenty-four tiers of shelves, perhaps a hundred jars per shelf, four walls. Using his forearms he pushed the ladder over to the corner beside the door and climbed it until he stood before the jar labeled in a plain script "Sample Number 1."

He stared at the hands inside the jar. They floated swollen and idle in the liquid, two grotesque deflating balloons. Near the bottom of the jar the liquid was less clear, a little murky. He tried to remember his hands. He could picture himself walking the wet roads, his legs splashed with water and mud, his face wet and dripping, his hair plastered flat. He could imagine himself in the house, the house raised on piles of stone to protect it from the rains, himself in the kitchen, his feet resting on the cracked lacquered chair, crossed at the ankles, near the stove's fire, his clothing hanging over the stove to dry, the soaked clothing letting fall cold drops on his bare feet and legs. But then—standing high on the ladder, one blunt-ended wrist hooked under a rung, the other resting on the highest tier—his memory uncrossed his ankles and edged the chair closer to the stove. He held out his arms to warm that at the end of them, found he could not envision hands but only the stumps he had now.

"How long has it been?" he wondered. "Did I ever have hands?"

He looked through the first line of jars, pushing flush against the back wall those that he was fairly certain did not belong to him. By looking at the stumps, the size of them, and holding them up to the side of the jar, he was able to discard quite a number, assuming the size was not distorted by glass and fluid. He would look into six or seven jars and then climb down, gripping the ladder with his forearms. He pushed the ladder forward several feet, then began again.

There were enough hands for a city, he thought. If they killed the people whose hands these were, what did they do with the bodies? Burn them, perhaps. He remembered each summer the roofs of the city outside becoming coated with a light ash. Each year people wondered where the ash came from, until rains came and cleared the roofs and people stopped wondering.

After an hour, he had lost the ability to differentiate between hands. There were small, obvious differences, true—a wart here, a twist in the finger there—but apart from that they seemed all the same. All had five fingers, all were sheared off at the wrist. He seemed to remember that his hands, like the rest of his skin, had been more pale than was common, but bloodless and in fluid all the hands were pale. He could not remember any scars on his hands, any irregularities, but that did not mean they had not been present. Perhaps there had been scars he had not noticed simply because he had possessed his hands too long.

He began to sort jars at random, to choose hands that could not possibly fit his wrists. He climbed down the ladder and pushed it back several hundred jars to pull out a jar he had pushed in a few minutes before. These are my beloved hands, he thought, hear them. If you bury hands, you must bury them deep enough that they cannot crawl to the surface. He closed his eyes his eyes an instant and saw on the walls of his skull a field, endless, sprouted with hands.

Nearing the end, he came to a jar that was empty, liquid in it but no hands. Blau stared at it. What if his hands had been in that jar and someone else had taken them? He imagined himself wandering the world in search of his hands, wandering from city to city, staring at people's wrists. He left the jar pulled out.

He began to leave out every other jar, moving quickly to the end. When he had finished, he moved the ladder back to the center of the room and sat down in the corner. With his stump he began to number the jars still pushed out that he had not yet eliminated. When he reached three hundred he stopped counting and sat down on the lowest rung of the ladder, resting his head on the blank ends of his wrists.

He got to his feet and climbed the ladder. He chose a jar, first taking one out, then another, not caring whether it was pushed against the wall or not, putting the first back, putting the second back, choosing a new jar altogether. Carefully he moved down the ladder, holding the jar wedged between his side and his arm, the other arm holding as best it could to the side of the ladder. He put the jar in the center of the room, and climbed the ladder again to get another. He imagined making a pyramid of jars in the center of the room.

The third jar he tried to bring down he dropped. The jar bounced then shattered, the hands sliding before shivering out and coming to rest. He did not care for the smell of formaldehyde. Blau found the empty jar in the shelves and brought it down, holding the jar with his knees and unscrewing the lid with his forearms, put the hands into it.

Finally, he had chosen ten jars for no particular reason and put them on the floor, one of those being the jar that had been empty. He walked around them, reading the labels. 24, 12, 8235, 1966, 812, 816, 725, 4996, 2. Without looking at the number, he picked up a jar and held it to his chest, his arms wrapped around it. He walked over to the door, kicked against it with his foot.

He hard the keys jingle, the guard curse. After a time, the door opened.

"What is it?" asked the guard.

"I have found my hands."

The guard reached into his breast pocket, removed a pair of glasses. He put them on, looked through them at the label of the jar. He removed them, put them away.

"No," he said, "these are not your hands," and shut the door.

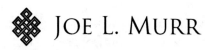 # Joe L. Murr
Fated

1. Bad Signs

He slits open the belly of a salmon and pulls out the guts. She hovers behind him, anxious. He examines the glistening entrails.

"The signs are hard to read," he says. "They suggest turbulent currents."

"Don't you see anything else?"

"The intestine is discolored. Here. And the bladder is distended. These are not auspicious signs."

He reaches out to her with messy hands.

She recoils from his touch. "Should we try the *I Ching* instead?"

He closes his eyes and throws yarrow stalks in his mind, interprets the hexagram. "There's a river. On the other side of the river, a man loses his goat. Between heaven and earth, the myriad creatures ... I can't go on."

Fish guts drop from his fingers.

She whispers, "I'm afraid. I'm afraid for us."

2. Young Love

Once upon a time, they caressed each other with the lubed-up tenderness of new lovers.

"It's written in the stars," he said.

"We're meant to be," she said.

He traced the lines of her palm. "It was fated."

"The first time I saw you, crows took flight behind you, flew in a figure eight. A snake on a rock ate its own tail. Then I knew."

"That it's forever. When we graduate ..."

She put a finger on his lips, snuggled in close. "Don't say it yet. I already know. Yes. I'll say yes."

"How did you know?"
"A little bird told me."

3. Infidelity

She'd lost count of all his late nights. Enough was enough. When he finally came home, she said, "This morning, I saw a dead cat in the dumpster."

"How terrible," he said, voice flat.

"It was swollen. Its fur crawled."

"What do you mean its fur crawled?"

"With fleas." She scratched her scalp. "It was an omen."

"How terrible."

"I scoured my skin. I scalded myself with hot water. I was in the bath for an hour."

"Terrible."

"My arms are covered in bites. I itched all day waiting for you to come back home. Why didn't you come home sooner?"

"I didn't know."

"You were with that girl."

"No."

"You were." She drew a symbol in the air to keep him honest. "You should've known I needed you here. Didn't you have tea with her?"

"I did."

"Then why didn't you see it in the tealeaves?"

His voice cracked with shame. "I used a teabag."

"How could you?"

He shuffled to the bedroom, sat at the end of the bed, face in his hands. She waited in the doorway for him to speak, the skin of her arms livid with fresh bites.

"I'm sorry," he said. He slapped the back of his neck. Something had bit him there. He held an insect between his fingers, watching its waving legs, then flicked it away. "Loose-leaf tea is messy. Inconvenient. She understands that."

"You should've told me."

"You should've known. Skried it in your crystal ball."

He packed clothing into a suitcase. She didn't try to stop him. Just watched. On his way out, he brushed bugs off his pants.

4. Reanimation

One night, he sleepwalked back to her. When he woke up, he found her snoring next to him in the bed they'd bought seven years ago from Ikea. His body was covered in capital letters written with red, black, and green magic markers. He must've done that in his sleep. The same word over and over again. TRUTH.

She exhaled deeply, put her arm around him. The gesture was comforting. It told him he was home.

They never spoke of his lover again.

5. Hopeless

Until now.

"It's not her again?" she says, unable to say her name.

He washes salmon gunk off his hands. "No. Haven't even thought of her for years."

"Maybe we should try something else." With a rising note of hope, she says, "I picked up old newspapers from the metro. There could be coded messages in the crossword puzzles."

"It's no use. We've tried everything. The answer's always the same. There's only one option."

"Yes? Anything."

"Purification. Meditate and fast for ten years."

"Too much. I can't."

"Me neither. It's no use at all."

He packs his bags, gives her his key.

6. Star-crossed

She posts a personal ad: "DWF VirgoGirl34 seeks Capricorn. The sun is in the Seventh House and Saturn in Libra."

He sees the ad, zaps off a reply: "Captain Capricorn knows the stars are right for love. Are you the one?"

Stephen McNally
IN MEMORIAM

Rabbit

Where does he come from?
He comes from a land where it is always raining.
Either that, or he was born in a time, in a place that does not exist,
and very likely has never existed.
For he has told me stories of the wild orange blossom, and of the towers
in the fabulous city made of ice.
And he sings (at night, when he thinks I am not listening)
of rivers which empty into the sky, and lakes of flowing gold,
and meadow grass made of light through which the devout can see
  the gods.

But where he came from is not so important.
More fascinating are the methods he used to travel here and to find me.
(You who don't believe, keep listening.) One day he imagined a cloud,
  and there was a cloud.
So he imagined a train, and a train pulled up before him.
Once inside, he imagined a railroad that shot into the fish eye of time, and
  there was a railroad.
He imagined a journey so impossible it would lead him to a land of hard
  bricks and gravity, and he found my world.
Then he imagined a man with blue rings of fire in his brain and he
  found me.

The days we have spent together!
Neither of us alone, for I tell him all the famous Bible stories
and explain the most obtuse scenes from Swedish movies.
I have whispered to him the secrets of Restoration Drama
and cooked fettuccini for him, and Greek meatballs.
And he has told me the fables of his country: how the three stone lions
　drove the demons from his land, how eagles rose out of the ground to
　breathe air into the sky,
and told me how his world was created from a single drop of water, a tear
　that fell from Heaven the day Hercules died.
From the tear came all of his world: the ice city, the circuses performed in
　clouds, the lamp posts set up in deserted fields and deep in forgotten
　forests so that spirits won't lose their way.

And you who don't believe,
don't think I believed at first. Don't think it was easy!
I was searching in a drugstore
for kitchen utensils and flashlight batteries on a January afternoon
when my rabbit found me.
I walked him home and he stood in a corner
for three days
before he spoke and told me what I'm telling you.

At first I took to heavy drinking, it all seemed so unreal.
Yet the more I drank, the larger he appeared to me, the more real he
　seemed.
I swallowed a combination of wild drugs,
saw purple badgers and floating mushrooms, but couldn't blot him from
　my vision.
He remained, calmly watching me.

Sober, I was about to take up religion
when, one evening, his words (for reasons you wouldn't understand)
  seemed reasonable and clear.
Like a waterfall, it all crashed down on me, but lovingly.
He was my friend, a real rabbit!
Someday a rabbit may find you.
But become worthy of them now.
Put aside the sweet notions of art and life you may have.
Rabbits care nothing for these things.
Art is a game played by killers
and life is nothing but swamp gas, a flash in the summer sky.

Then, someday
you may be walking along thinking
"ice cream, walnuts, bank accounts, toothpaste" or noticing
the soft outline of a woman's breast beneath her sweatshirt
or just hating the people who live next door
when you find yourself in a part of town you've never seen,
pulling a couple of bills from your pocket
and walking into a pet store
where they're having a sale on long-eared, short-tailed burrowing
  mammals with soft fur.

Moon

The murderer appeared at my doorstep in the night and he was dazzling,
 his eyes two vaults guarded by ageless, chanting priests.
As I stared at him the snow hurried closer to touch his coat
and the moon covered us with his red hands.

With her red hands the moon covered us
and the lightning bolts which had traveled since August found their way
 into the ground again,
making the earth glow
as if the dead were building fires.
"The dead are building fires," the murderer said.

His voice came from a hollow place near a distant lake
and the snow hanging on his black coat
formed the star chart for a galaxy beyond our reach.

I felt like the shadow of someone walking slowly through a forest in the
 dead of winter
or like the memory hanging in the air after the foghorn has sounded
as he sat beneath the window
and spoke to it: "Soon they will forget us entirely. Already they are
 building fires."

I said prayers in a language I had never heard
and in my mind a tiny attic door at the top of a staircase slammed shut
as I sat with him and watched
the snow dance against the wind,
the silent branches grope into the night
and the moon cover everything with her red hands.

REVIEW OF *CHILD IN AMBER*

Stephen McNally's *Child of Amber* won the 1992 Juniper Prize from the University of Massachusetts Press. It's his sole collection, as the poet, a graduate of the Iowa Writer's Workshop and Professor in the Southern Methodist University English Department for eight years, passed away in 1998, but it is a treasure trove of most stunning poems. Open this book and you'll encounter paginated enchantment, a poetic cabinet of curiosities, marvels, and "velvet fairy tales" (as Jack Myers aptly suggests on the back cover), all craftily put to music and impeccable lineation.

McNally's speakers supplant reality with a deft surrealism. *Child of Amber*'s last poem and final section is entitled "The Message," and readers should be prepared to hear some amazing messages indeed throughout this book: the premonitions of a seer through the voice of a witness to an apocalypse ("Among the Ruins"), "the rush of air and ecstatic hush of the audience" which nearly makes the nostalgia of a trapeze artist real ("Evening of the Trapeze Artist"), and even cryptic messages delivered through beautiful tattoos which truly move (The Stars and the Beautiful Tattooed Man"). McNally upholds a standard of clarity and economy of language many poets who resist imaginary content don't maintain. Such surreal flair and devoted craft combined with an eye for discovery leave imaginary ideas tantalizingly real.

Fascinating also in terms of history, *Child of Amber* places worlds that no longer exist but that may have existed long ago at the reader's fingertips. "Report from the Interior" follows a party of explorers searching for a "golden city" who discover how precarious life can be as their comrades disappear into sinister jungle surroundings. The lines themselves lengthen and the tone grows increasingly ominous just as the jungle does for these men, "who lose sight of scouts the moment they advance ten paces..."

McNally's stylistic penchant for extended line, anaphora, and exclamation on occasion seems reminiscent of Whitman, but his is a singular voice and sensibility. Those scouring American Poetry for a profoundly original love poem, for instance, might do no better than the flights of the lines in "Heavenly:"

> If I were a mad Italian Conductor,
> I would twist several languorous symphonies
> into existence for you,
> and all the gnarled trees and all the lovely ruins along the Via Appia,
> would lie down,
> and even the gulls crouched as far as Seal Rock would hear it
> and be transfixed for an instant
> by memories of picnicking lovers they had seen
> during aimless flights over California beaches.

The poet's gentle treatment of animals may endear readers as well. Creatures seem to flock to Stephen McNally's poems as if they're a refuge. During "Olmec Head," dolphins nuzzle the hulls of ships where octopi are allowed "on board." "In the cool, dark jungles giraffes are eating pineapples," the poet writes in "Sentenced," whose speaker has been ordered to concoct a line by a demanding young friend named "Cleveland." "Procession" conceals a salamander who "sleeps blue and sooty under a young man's arm," and at the close of "Beautiful Child," a "sick hippopotamus" is allowed to rest after years of dancing at a children's circus. The vibrancy and color of living things resides in these poems, which seem almost to breathe and to lead imaginative lives as natural as the lives of the creatures they shelter.

For those who prefer to remain in human company, McNally explores our world too deeply to be considered escapist. Much of what Federico Garcia Lorca called *duende* lives here. Many poems confront disappointment, death, and/or despair: "Our Story," "Grief for the Living," and "Human Pursuits" among them. Ultimately, however, *Child of Amber* marshals its readers as "the tourists and curious countrymen" briefly mentioned at the end of "Heavenly," who are allowed "to see just what the ancients thought of our souls' possibilities." These poems are meant to lead us toward "the new life, where the mysteries we ignore in this one / will finally be revealed."

Matt Schumacher, July 2011

Geronimo G. Tagatac
Counting

The tiny woman in the back of my head sings me to sleep at night in her scratchy voice. While I dream, she tracks my heartbeats and when she reaches about thirty thousand, she wakes me by putting her tiny index finger against the inside of my head and pushing. Then she softens the darkness in my room until my eyelids flutter. I open my eyes and it's 5:15AM. For twenty minutes, I lie in my bed and let the rhythm of my pulse and the counter-rhythm of my breath soak all the way down my arms and legs. With my fingers, I trace the seam of the scar that goes from just below my neck, down the middle of my chest, to the top of my stomach to where it meets the other seam to form a cross just below my ribcage where the two drainage tubes once exited my torso.

As I sit up slowly, and there's the sliver of a thought that the seams formed by the scars might not hold, that I might burst open, staining the sheets and the comforter with a sudden rush of blood internal organs. But I know better because it's been a year and a half since the surgeons closed and fastened my chest together. I rise and go into the bathroom and step into a hot shower. The water drums against the top of my head and my shoulders and I'm suddenly in Kowloon, though I don't know how I know this. I am running in an afternoon downpour along the north-south rail-line. The warm rain has soaked me to the skin. My t-shirt is plastered to my torso and my running shoes make a faint squishing sound each time they hit the wet earth. My chest scars have disappeared. The tops of the nearby trees writhe in the wind of an oncoming typhoon. I could run forever.

When I finish toweling off, I make a mark on the side of the bathroom door with the pencil that hangs from a string, line my pills up on the bathroom counter and begin taking them, chasing each with a swallow of water. There are twenty-seven marks on the doorframe, one for each vision I've had. I have never been to Kowloon.

By the time I roll my bike out of the garage and pedal across the park, the sun is painting the oaks with yellow-green light from their tops down. Beneath the canopy of the trees, I enjoy the soft the sound of my tires on the leaf-covered earth and the vibration of the handlebars in my hands and arms, until I reach High Street.

It's 6:30AM when I reach The Blue Gila Café. I use my key to open the thick wood door with its arched glass window that's painted with a mottled blue Gila monster lizard beneath the café's name. I push the door open gently, without touching the painted reptile. It's early and the thing might not like being startled. I lock the door behind me and go back to the office to retrieve the till and turn on the XM Radio sound system. I pull the scones from the refrigerator and put them in the oven. Then I start the coffee brewers and nod good morning to Lulu, the chrome-and-red Ostoria espresso machine, with its three spouts and wands waiting patiently to make the first drinks of the day. I take chairs off the tables. Then I carry the twelve metal chairs out to the sidewalk, where I set up the folding tables. Before I go back into The Gila, I look up to the east. The sun is still below the line of buildings across the street.

With the soft blue light streaming up behind them, the buildings could be a painted plywood backdrop on a stage. At any moment, men in close-fitting suits will strut onto the sidewalk and execute a series of dance steps as they break into song.

When I walk back through the door of The Gila, I collide with the strong smell of freshly brewed coffee. It reminds me of the cubicle warren that I worked in until after my surgery, and the brown water that posed as the real thing. At The Gila, we use nothing but the highland grown Arabica beans. None of that lowland Robusto that goes into the two-pound discount cans on supermarket shelves.

At five to seven, I unlock the door. Brinley, Andrea and Sully have been standing there for a ten minutes wearing faces that I've seen in black-and-white photos of about-to-be-liberated concentration camp inmates staring through barbed wire. I hold the door open for them and then walk behind the counter, where I pour medium-sized mugs of house blend for Brinley and Sully, leaving room in Brinley's for cream, and slide them across the counter beside the register. I take their money, make change and turn to the espresso machine. I hear the clink of change hitting the bottom of the tip jar, which reminds me of that tiny voice that sang me to sleep in the night. I pull a shot, tamp it, lock the basket into Lulu, slide a cup under the spout and punch the high strength button. I froth some milk, pour the hot milk into the cup, holding back the foam till last and wait for something to show itself on the foam's surface. I'm not disappointed.

It's begins as a faint discoloration, as the thin layer of caffeine, the crema, stains its way through the center of the foam's center. It starts as a crescent that bleeds a delicate line, then another, and then another until I'm looking down at the profile of a young woman's face. She has curly hair falling past where her shoulders would be and her lips are parted. The image darkens, gains more definition. The face turns slowly toward me. I reached down quickly with a tiny espresso spoon, before Andrea can see what I'm doing, stir it through the face, turn and slide the cup and saucer across the counter to Andrea. "Neat!" she says. I look down at the cappuccino's surface. The face is gone, replaced by the silhouette of a fleeing dog trailing an ownerless leash.

"Like that?" I say, as she hands me two crisp ones.

"How'd you do it?" she replies as I hand her her change.

"Totally random," I tell her.

"Looks like Carter."

"The ex-president?" I ask, wondering if the cappuccino has become a Rorschach blot that looks different to each of us."Neighbor's dog."

I look into her brown eyes and nod. She turns and I hear the sharp rhythm of her no-nonsense shoes against the dark fir floor as she walks away without tipping. Perhaps she thinks I've just handed her a cup of dishonesty with a shot of sarcasm. Or maybe she thinks that I know more about her life than I'm letting on. It's a small town. I lower my wrist below the counter and check my pulse with the first two fingers of my right hand. No change. It's a calm sixty-nine throbs a minute. My heart registers no embarrassment or unhappiness at Andrea's annoyance. "Why so cool?" I ask it.

At noon, I turn things over to Nick and, with a cup of Moroccan mint tea, make my way up the creaky stairs to the break room, where I try to avoid being swallowed by the ancient, thrift store couch while I take my second series of medications, including the cyclosporin that suppresses my immune system that keeps it from rejecting the heart that I received, a year and a half ago. I sit back into the cushions and the taste of mint is hot and sharp against my tongue. It works its way through the roof of my mouth, into my sinuses and the front of my head, just behind my eyes.

I lie back and close my eyes. I'm on a huge plaza. It's morning and the ground fog turns the plaza into a grainy photograph. A man on a bicycle rides out of the fog past me. Two people in striped, hooded robes hurry by and vanish into the mist. And then the whole scene is sucked into a deeper fog and I am back in the shabby break room. I open my eyes. The break room's walls are papered with garage band posters for the "Dirty Tricks," "Benzedrine," "End Time Party" and "Monkey Whackers," that are a record of almost a decade of local teen angst. I look up at the felt pen sign that proclaims, "No drugs in break room." I smile and swallow the last of my meds, chasing them down with the last three inches of my tea.

I'm back behind the counter when Creaky Lon comes in carrying his red and white gym bag. Lon has this habit of hanging his dozen or so handball gloves to dry from a carabiner hooked to the D-ring at the bag's end. The gloves are withered and pale and I've seen people on the street do double takes when he walks by, thinking that Lon's a dangerous weirdo who collects amputated right hands. He wears a fanny pack with the pouch, facing front, under a Hawaiian shirt that makes him look eight-and-a-half months pregnant. Lon lowers the big bag gently onto the floor beside a table, pulls up the front of his shirt with its bright tropical flower pattern to get at the money in his fanny pack. For a moment I have this image of him reaching into an opening in a rain forest where his torso should be and withdrawing a worn leather wallet handed to him by something or someone I can't see. "Latte and scone?" I say, as he hands me a five-dollar bill. He nods. I pop the cash register, give him his change, pull the shot, lock the basket, hit the six-second button and say, "Give me a strong one, Lulu." Under one of the wands, I steam some milk in an i-brick, a small stainless steel pitcher and the warm dairy smell hisses up to fill my nose.

"Latte and a scone," I call and watch Lon make his way to the counter. The way he walks, you'd think his hips and lower back were made of glass. So how does he manage to play so much handball? The guy must be pushing seventy. I'm thirty years younger than him and I probably suck down five times the meds he's taking.

I feel a movement of air against the left side of my face and catch a whiff of cigarette smoke. I look up to see Mila pushing through the door with her left arm. Her right hand caresses the lizard's back, though she pulls it away quickly when I glance up at her. She's wearing a short, muted orange-patterned dress over the top of a pair of pre-faded jeans. Its color compliments her French-braided red-brown hair, which hangs in a thick rope over her left shoulder. Mila started coming in three months ago, when she and her husband split up. She's dressed down today. She's usually togged out in one of her dark pantsuits and matching leather shoes. Maybe she's given up on trying to find a job.

"What'll it be, Mila?" I ask.

"Double latte," she replies without making eye contact. She reaches into her blue bag and pulls out a wallet that's fat with credit cards and photos, reaches into it, slips out a twenty and lays it on the counter. I slide her change halfway across the counter to her then and turn to pull the shot, knowing that I won't hear the ring of change in the tip jar. The first time I tried handing her change to her she winced. Since then I've avoided the merest hint of physical proximity. The word around The Gila is that she's in the middle of divorce proceedings that would make the Rwandan genocide look like a polite disagreement between two people over what kind of breakfast cereal to buy.

    I pour steamed milk over two shots of espresso and wait. A brown stain spreads across the white surface of Mila's drink and jells into the silhouette of a centipede. By the time I put the tall glass mug onto the counter, it's become a blurred S. "Double latte!" I call and watch Mila's shoulders hunch slightly and relax again. She could be a large, flightless bird flapping her stunted wings. I slide the tall glass mug halfway across the counter and, when she reaches the counter, I say, "Anything thing else? I just pulled a fresh batch of scones out of the oven." Mila looks down at her latte and then up at me, her amber colored eyes varnished with skepticism. Maybe she thinks I picked up the pastries at a big box store. The line of her mouth turns into a shallow U then goes back to a thin, straight incision between her lips. It makes me think of the scar bisecting my upper torso. Mila shakes her head once with a quick, sharp movement that's little more than a twitch that pulls her face out of focus for a hundredth of a second. Then she hoists her drink and walks back to her table with a stride that makes me wonder if she's had a anti-sway bar installed alongside her hips. The woman's a walking candidate for a total body root canal job.

    At eleven, Dejay comes in to cover my lunch break. She blasts through the door in a jumble of dance steps. She turns with the door, making the painted lizard into a dance partner, whirling him around and flinging him off to crash against the doorstop nailed to the floor. The light behind Dejay sparkles off the multiple rings in the piercings that rim both her ears. She waves a tattooed arm at me and yells, "Hallo, comrades! Another day to shine for the poor, the socially inept, the sleep laden and the unfashionable!" Everyone in the place looks up, except for Mila, who slams her cell phone shut, takes a swallow of her latte and makes for the door, giving Dejay a parting look that could cut glass. Dejay whirls around the counter, dances up to me, does a quick spin, pulls me to her and partners me out of the narrow space in a mock tango, arms pointing, Groucho Marx crouch stepping, switching arms, reversing direction until we reach the other end of the café. She pushes me through a turn beneath her left arm, releases me and says, "Don't do drugs, take your meds and always remember to wear clean socks, Emelio."

    I pour myself a cup of green tea and go out to the sidewalk. Above the buildings on the other side of Glide Street, the clouds are a gray ceiling a few hundred feet up. I stand there and try to recall what the sky looked like in my dream but the sound of cars streaming by and the feel of the humidity against the skin of my forearms and face crowd out everything else. The lunch crowd streams past me, mostly twentysomethings with tidy office hairdos and leather shoes. "Firsters," Dejay calls them: first jobs, first cars, first apartments. I'm sure that some of them have tattoos stamped discretely below the collar lines of their cotton shirts or silk blouses or at the bases of their spines. Many of the guys sport the ubiquitous barbed wire strands tattooed around one of their upper arms under the sleeves of their oxford cloth dress shirts. The thin aroma of aftershave lotion and perfume forms a moving cloud around them. This post-operative sensitivity to smell makes me wonder if I might have been given the heart of a dog.

I glance into those bright faces and wonder if the young man whose heart keeps me alive resembled any of them. All that I'm permitted to know was that he was nineteen when he did a bad job of shooting himself in the head one night. Perhaps he listened to the same voice that I hear at night, singing him into oblivion as his brain activity shrank to a firefly-sized glow. I try to imagine him, lying in the antiseptic light of the ER, the ventilator breathing for him, his heart running on and on, waiting for his parents to make a choice and to sign the papers that would send a surgical team in to remove his heart, kidney, liver, eyes, to take his bone and skin tissue, to finish with scalpels what he'd started with a bullet.

I don't suppose that the light in ER was very different than the light in my old office cubicle.

When my shift is done, at three, I walk down to the YMCA and change into running gear. I jog south, past the creek and into the park. The oaks and maples tower up and blot out the sky above the narrow path that winds through knee high grass. The occasional breeze combs the topmost leaves in the trees ruffling their calm. The rhythm of my breath and the sound of my running shoes against the packed earth expand until they fill the space beneath the green canopy. Twenty-nine months ago, this is where my chest tightened and my breath shortened. That's when all of the greens, yellows and earth colors did this swirl, faded to gray and stayed that way. For weeks after I began to run again, I avoided this part of the park, afraid that its shadows would stain my new heart or that I might see something in my peripheral vision the size and shape of a badger, making sudden rushes and halts, a dark shape half hidden in the purple camas, pacing me.

There is nothing here this afternoon but the smell of earth, leaves and grass, only the blue shards of sky between the branches of the treetops and the rustle of a squirrel panicked at my approach. Before me, the trail falls away to the far edge of the trees, becoming a slack line down which I run toward the band of yellow light at the tree line's far edge. Though I'm tempted to look down at my feet, I keep my head up and my eyes focused fifty yards in front of me, trusting in the wisdom of my legs the way that a dancer is taught not to look down at his feet. The cadence of my footfalls rises up and drowns my thoughts.

In the health club, I stand under the shower and listen to the sound the water makes against the top of my head and wonder what Penny, my former wife, is doing. I see her standing before me in the shower, the water running through her blond hair, darkening it and molding it to the sides of her face, accentuating her cheekbones. Her hands are on my shoulders and mine hold her hips. It is late morning and we have just made love. Nothing exists but the light blue of her eyes. And then the water washes her away and I'm standing alone in the white tiled shower room recalling that I haven't been married for nearly two years because Penny couldn't bear the idea of living with a man who has to take more than a dozen meds every day, a husband who could die any time his body decided to reject its own heart. Penny was thirty-six years old and she'd already watched me dying for nearly a year before the transplant. The reasonable part of me can't blame her. Another part of me wants to put a king cobra into her warm sheets while she sleeps beside her boyfriend, Klein. A snake for snakes.

That night, I dream that I'm in the park again where death first said, "Hey." The moon has frozen the colors from the trees and grass. Something in the woods has reached into my chest and is pulling me forward. I am crumbling an anise biscotti between my thumb and forefinger, dropping the crumbs onto the path, which Mila, who follows me, stops to retrieve and put into her mouth. The breeze is at my back and it carries the smell her skin and the scent of her hair even though she's behind me. Why does she have no smell at The Blue Gila?

I stop at a broad pond that shouldn't be in the park and throw the last of the biscotti onto its surface. The reflections of the moon and stars ripple. When I kneel and put my hand into the water it's so cold that frost forms on my forearm. Mila kneels beside me and puts her hand on my right forearm. I bend, put my face to the water and drink. The stars and the moon slide into my mouth and down my throat. The taste is bitter and so cold that my throat and chest grow brittle. When I pull my face away from the pond's surface Mila is no longer beside me. I see her walking into the darkness. Someone is behind her.

I run to warn her. Behind me, the wind rises. It carries the aroma of strong coffee that wakes the birds and sets them singing wildly. The smell of espresso erases Mila's aromatic signature. I don't like the way this dream is going, so I reach forward with my right arm and throw it to the right while springing upward with my legs. I feel my feet separate from the ground as I turn upward. The tops of the camas brush against my shoe soles as I fly past the tree trunks, turning over in the darkness. Leaves brush clockwise against my face, and then I'm above the treetops. The moon pulls me into the night sky. The cold air numbs my fingers. But the inertia of my earthbound heart is a lead weight at the bottom of my chest. At any moment it will tear itself lose from its connecting arteries and leave my lifeless body to vanish into the sky's black dome, leaving a cascade of blood.

I wake in the middle of my bed, which the moonlight has transformed into white pool. In my mouth, a bitter taste. My heart is a fist hammering the inside of my chest. "Hey! Hey! Knock it off," I tell it.

In the morning, when I go down to The Blue Gila, Mila is standing on the sidewalk, waiting for me to open the place. "Morning," I say. She nods, rummages around in her purse and pulls out a crumpled blue pack of foreign brand cigarettes. Mila's feet do this little shuffling dance. Right, left, right, together. Left, right, left, together. I'm tempted to ask her if she'd like to sneak in while I'm opening and use the women's room. "You okay?" I ask.

"Didn't sleep," she replies, actually making eye contact with me. Her voice is that of an asthmatic and the puffiness around her eyes makes me wonder if she's spent the night screaming over the phone at her ex-husband. "Come on. I'll make you a double shot before I open up. You can sit on the couch that faces away from the windows," I tell her. She nods, follows me through the door, which I lock behind her. She doesn't even flinch when the deadbolt clacks into place but heads straight for the dark green couch and its shapeless cushions.

I empty a pound of Italian dark roast into the grinder, hit the on switch and watch Mila as the grating sound fills the place. Her shoulders remain level. I fill the ground coffee dispenser, pull two shots, tamp them, lock them onto the machine and hit the extra-strong button. I should be fetching the till and taking chairs off the tables. Instead, I watch the espresso fall thinly into the cups beneath the spouts, remembering the black surface of the pond in my dream and the cold taste of the stars. Then I pour them both into a small cup, put it on a saucer with a tiny spoon and two sugar cubes. Rather than call the order, I walk it over to Mila. She's lying back against the sofa cushion, her eyes closed. I sit on the edge of the sofa across from her, hold out the espresso and say, "Hey," in a soft voice.

Mila's eyelids open and she stares at the white cup and saucer the way that she might look at a small UFO hovering in front of her face, trying to come to terms with the reality of the thing, eliminating any other possibilities. I'm tempted to laugh but I restrain myself.

Maybe she's suffering from short-term memory loss. I put the drink down on the tiles of the coffee table and slide it over to her the way I'd push a scrap of food to a wary, stray dog. That's when I notice that her clothes aren't her. The crispness and complimentary colors are missing. She's wearing an oversized, bleached out gray sweatshirt over a baggy pair of overalls. She's pulled her hair back into a greasy ponytail with a rubber band. I can't decide if Mila's having a very butch morning or just gotten a job with a roofing crew.

She takes a couple of minutes to rummage through all the overall pockets before coming up with a one-dollar bill that she puts onto the table and runs the palm of her hand over it, trying to take a few years off of George Washington's face. Before she can look up, I say, "My treat, Mila." Then I get up to retrieve the till.

"Are you one of those nice guys? You know I'm not one of those women in distress," Mila says not unkindly.

When I turn to face her, I have the impression that I'm looking at her through a reversed set of binoculars. "You never struck me as the gothic novel heroine," I reply.

"What do I strike you as, Emilio?"

"I never thought about it much, but now that I do, I picture you as the non-fiction, ten-minute manager twelve-step investment program person." I reply, smiling.

The morning's first regulars are gathering beyond The Gila's door, including Creaky Lon with his collection of hands. He's wearing white knee socks, green high top tennis shoes and favoring his left leg. "To be continued," I say and head for the door with my key.

I fill everyone's orders, one latte, a single shot and two brewed Italian roasts with room for cream. Then I look over at the couch. Mila's gone. Over the sound system, Hugh Masekela's, "Grazing in the Grass" puts out its brassy sound. Mila's white cup and saucer sit in the middle of the table. Maybe all that concentrated caffeine blasted her out the door. She might be embarrassed about talking with me. She could have vanished into the cup. When I go over to take the cup away, I see that she's left the dollar bill as a tip. I pick it up and turn it back and forth, looking for a clue as to what's going on with Mila. But the president's faded green face stares back at me impassively. So I take the bill and drop it into the tip jar where it lies atop the quarters and dimes for the rest of the morning. No one seems to feel as generous as Mila today.

"Oh please, please, please say you love me!" Says Dejay, leaning over the counter so low that her earrings make scratchy noises against the polished wood.

"You're such a tramp. What do want?"

"Say you'll take my closing shift."

"When?"

Dejay's olive skinned hand reaches out faster than a striking krait, seizes my wrist and pulls me halfway across the counter. Her other arm reaches around the back of my head and pulls me to within an inch of her dark eyes. Her hair smells of cinnamon incense. "Tonight," she breathes. Before I can react, she kisses me full on the mouth.

"You never told me you were bi, Dejay," I say when she lets me up for air.

"Only for you. C'mon, Emilio, there's this girl..."

"You've got a girlfriend."

"I broke it off with Elissa two weeks ago."

"What? Did her expiration date come up or did you get tired of her tattoos?"

Her fingers tighten on the back of my head. "It's not a good idea to taunt a desperate woman."

"I can't take your shift if I'm injured or dead."

"You're heartless," she says, releasing me.

"Not technically speaking. But having someone else's pump does give one a sense of proportion, Dejay." I gently pull her arms away from around my neck. "You'll owe me for this one." I pour myself a glass of water and go to the break room to take my meds.

The sidewalk in front of The Blue Gila is swirling with people when I return, at six. I wade through the crowd of mostly underage smokers and a few older, homeless hangers on. I try to come up with the theme party names for the scene: "Suburban Weltschmerz" and "Ennui for the Inexperienced."

"Yo, Emilio!" It's Johnny, wearing mid-calf camouflage patterned shorts, flip-flops, a linked belt of what I hope are inactive M-60 machine gun rounds around his hips and a black hoodie. His dyed black hair hangs in shoulder-length dreadlocks. He's my height and a few pounds heavier than me. Maybe nineteen years old. The word is that he's spent the last year couch surfing since his parents threw him out of the house.

"Hey, Johnny," I say, wondering if he's going to hit me up for another free mocha. The washed out blue of the kid's eyes make me wonder if he's on something, but his clothes don't give off the odor of someone who's just done weed and the darker pupils of his eyes aren't dilated beyond normal. At nineteen, he's used up nearly seven-hundred million of his allotted heart beats, unless something steps out of the shadows, puts its hand over his face, stops his breath and puts him to sleep. "Can I get you anything?" I ask. "It's on me."

Johnny smiles softly and the blue of his eyes deepens. "Oh hey, way cool, Emilio.

Americano okay?" He follows me past the door's rampant blue lizard. He's lugging a sleeping bag tied to a gym bag.

"Where you living these days, Johnny?"

"Mind if I use the bathroom to wash up?" He asks, answering my question.

"Go ahead," I say, sliding the key attached to a ratty, child's stuffed skunk toy to him. "But don't be too long at it or Dave's gonna' wonder what's going on. Besides, your drink will get cold," I tell him as I make my way to the espresso machine.

"I'm down with that," he says, walking off with the skunk hanging from his right hand. I remind myself to find out how long skunks live. They last longer in captivity that in the wild, I guess, but then they don't like captivity any more than Johnny liked living with parents.

As I brew the espresso for Johnny's Americano, I wonder how Dejay's doing on her date. And what about Mila? Maybe she's sitting on her couch watching a sitcom and fuming about the missing stereo that her soon to be ex-husband took when he left, or about the years that they spent together that she might have used to get an MBA or a law degree. Judging from the way she looked, Mila's likely zonked out on anti-depressants and half a bottle of white wine, a comatose woman sprawled in the middle of a king-sized mattress, her pulse the only thing keeping her afloat.

Johnny appears at the counter and slides the stuffed skunk with the bathroom key over to me and I slide the double Americano over to him. "What're you up to, tonight?" I ask.

"There's a party at Jeffrey's later."

"Yeah? Where's that?"

"Nineteenth Street on the other side of Court. Him, Dejay and Tim share the place," Johnny says.

"Didn't know Dejay lived there."

"Five months. Sometimes she lets me couch surf for a couple of nights in exchange for cleaning up the place," he says, picking up his coffee and heading for the door.

"Who's Dejay's latest love interest?" I call out to him.

"Some straight type named Mona or Mila," Johnny says before vanishing beyond the blue Gila monster, leaving me with the image of Mila in her thrift store chic leisure wear, drink in hand, leaning against Dejay on a broken down couch, which seems a happier alternative to my earlier image of her. As I wipe down the counter with a damp towel, I wonder how long a relationship between a lapsed heterosexual divorcee on the rebound and Dejay can last.

"Double espresso with a twist of lemon peel," says a familiar voice. It's my ex-wife.

"What brings you to this side of the world?" I ask, with what I hope is a neutral tone of voice and a blank face.

"Starbucks isn't open this late," she replies, giving me the once over with the gray eye on the left side of her face. A smile softens the line of her mouth. Her blond hair is has grown past her shoulders and it's lighter than I recall.

I pull two shots of espresso, lock the basket onto the machine, push the button for the strongest setting and put a small white cup under the spout. I watch the black thread slide from the chrome lip. It pools up in the cup's bottom, making the porcelain look whiter than it did seconds before. I'm actually sorry that Penny didn't order a cappuccino or breve. I'd like to see the image that would appear in her coffee. I put the cup onto a saucer and put a thin curl of lemon rind and a tiny spoon there as well. As I slide the black, yellow, chrome and white thing that I've created across the counter, I realize that it's more substantial than anything I might have done at my office job, or perhaps in my marriage to this woman.

"There you are," I say.

"I had to ask around to find out where you were working," Penny says without a trace of annoyance in her voice.

"I'm moving in a different professional circle now."

"How's your health?" she asks, meaning my heart.

"Takes a licking and keeps on ticking, as long as I take my meds and watch what I eat."

"You've lost weight."

"Good excuse for a new wardrobe."

"You mean a downgrade," Penny replies, taking in my jeans and t-shirt.

"Are you still seeing Klein?"

She breaks the lemon peel twist in two and drops one of the pieces into her espresso. "We decided to stop dating. We had issues," she says. The line of her mouth flattens into a straight line and she takes a tiny, careful sip of coffee. "Not bad. A shame you didn't know how to do this before we separated."

"For two-sixty I'll make you a double anytime you want it," I reply, smiling.

Penny looks back at me and laughs. It's a soft sound that rises to a short hoot.

"This one's on me," I say, thinking that If I keep this up I'm going to have return half my salary to Dave.

"Why'd you leave your job, Emilio?"

"It just didn't seem important anymore."

"You had everything."

"I had an eight-by-ten cubicle and the promise of a promotion."

She takes another sip of caffeine. "It was good money, benefits and a retirement plan."

I remember the number that I came up with after my recovery. "Six-hundred and twenty-nine million."

"What?"

"The number of heartbeats until I could have retired," I say. "Seventeen years."

Her mouth opens then closes. "Besides you, who's counting, Emilio?"

"You want to know if I think this is an improvement," I say.

Penny reaches down for her tiny cup but her thumb collides with its handle, knocking it sideways. She reaches down quickly and rights the tiny cup, but it's too late. The last sip of coffee and its dregs are a jagged brush stroke across the counter's dark surface. "Oh shit! I'm sorry," she says. I look down at the cup, at the yellow sliver of lemon peel and the arc of espresso reaching across the polished wood, trying to photograph it, to freeze it forever in my mind. In this moment, I realize that I could never have willfully created such a composition in a million years. I may never see such a thing again.

I look up at Penny and ask, "Did you ever go to Europe?"

"Klein and I went to Rome a month before we called it quits. We fought the last three days we were there."

"You always wanted to see the Pantheon."

"Yes," she says, looking down at the splash of espresso.

"Don't worry about it. Happens all the time."

"Why'd you let me leave you? You never tried to stop me."

"I didn't know how long I'd live after the transplant. You wanted to get on with your life. I don't think you'd have liked having a forty-five year old barista as a life partner." Then I say, "Besides, you were already sleeping with Klein."

Then she does something I've never seen her do: she turns her face down and starts to cry. "I'm sorry, I'm sorry," she whispers.

I'm tempted to reach over the counter and put my hand over hers, but I don't. "It's not your fault, Penny."

She looks up at me. "What if..."

"Let me get you something else."

"I have to go, Emilio," she says, extracting a small package of tissues from her purse, pulling one free and blotting the corners of her gray eyes.

I watch Penny gather herself together, pulling her feelings back behind her pale eyes and smooth forehead, until she seems denser and harder than she was a moment before. "Goodbye," she says as she stands and makes a smooth quarter-pirouette that I remember so well from our nights on the Sapphire Club dance floor. And then she's striding up to the alarmed lizard on the door, pulling it aside and sliding quickly past its outstretched blue claws. And then Penny's gone, past the swirling teens into night.

There's nothing for me to do but to wipe away the spilled espresso with a damp dishtowel and put the empty cup and saucer into a bus tray. Deep in the center of my chest, there's something heavy and cold. Maybe it's something Penny left behind that's made its way into my new heart. We've been divorced for nearly two years. I wonder if she expected me to survive this long. It's nine-thirty. Time to start closing. Outside, the kids are still milling, talking and smoking but their numbers have thinned. Johnny's gone.

By the time I get home, the tinny voice has been singing in the back of my head for nearly an hour. She's anxious to start her count. She's doing a scratchy love song about the fall wind blowing through streets of Paris. I line up my meds on the counter beside the bathroom sink and look at the reflection of myself in the mirror. The face staring back at me is utterly different than the one I knew three years before, with its tired eyes and gray-brown complexion. This is the face of another man, the eyes a clear brown, the chin strong and firm and the cheekbones firm. They are the eyes that I've seen staring back at me from a Raphael fresco. The lines at the corner of the eyes are subtle marks of authority and experience rather than scars of fatigue. I punctuate each swallowed pill with a swallow of water, brush my teeth and get into bed.

I close my eyes and find myself back at The Blue Gila. But the blue lizard is missing from its place on the glass door. It's crawling along the top of the coffee bar, claws tapping and scrabbling on the slick surface, leaving deep scratches in the dark wood. I chase it down the bar, reaching for the end of its thrashing tail, but it stays just out of reach. Just when I think it must stop or topple off the bar's end, the bar lengthens until it's a narrow highway that goes past the espresso machine and the small dishwasher, all the way through the kitchen. The counter's end bursts through the café's back door with the lizard right behind it and me chasing the reptile which is carrying my heart between its jaws. Now I'm running as hard as I can because I know that if I don't catch that blue scribble, I'm going to die. I chase the thing out the back door, my lungs screaming for air and muscles of my thighs and calves are might as well have been dipped in acid. The lizard is widening his lead.

I gasp and sit up in my bed. My heart is banging away to the cadence of my breath, back where it should be, behind the cage of scars on my chest. I look around, expecting to see the Gila monster, glowing blue in the darkness, waiting to make another grab for my heart. "Go back to your door!" I yell, just in case he's hiding under the bed or crouched in the space between the dresser and the wall. I listen for the sound of a whispery hiss. There is nothing but the kitchen sound of the refrigerator pushing fluid through its cold interior. I lie back into my warm sheets and pull the comforter over my chest. Above me, the ceiling is a snowy expanse. I wonder if I should tell the members of my heart transplant support group about all of this.

The next morning, I wake late and swallow my meds two and three at a time. The lizard on the door is waiting for me when I walk up to the café. I unlock the door, reach out and give the back of its head a nasty shove with the palm of my right hand. "Thief!" I say. The lizard and the door swing out of my way. Inside, I relock the door and start taking chairs off of tables. Within ten minutes, the usual group has formed, but I don't look up at them. I pull a shot and tamp it, lock the basket and hit the full strength button. I haven't had a brewed cup of coffee in eighteen months, much less a full-strength double shot. It's not recommended, but I don't care. I bring down the till, put out the pastries and walk over to the door. I'd like to slap the grin off of the thieving lizard's jaws. I notice that his skin has faded to a lighter blue, which calms me a bit as I slide my key into the lock and turn the deadbolt counterclockwise and pull the door open.

Mila's standing there, looking at me with her dark eyes. She's dressed in high-heeled, knee-length black boots, a black pencil skirt and a fitted gray leather jacket over a blue silk blouse. "Let me repay you for yesterday," she says.

"Don't worry about it," I reply, holding the door open for her.

Mila walks over to the counter and pulls herself onto a stool. "You know, you're not a bad guy underneath that cool layer you wear."

I pull a double shot and tamp it, lock the basket and punch the espresso machine button. Then I turn to her, wanting to say, "My ex-wife was in yesterday. I haven't seen her in nineteen months. I signed the divorce papers from a post-op recovery room." But I say nothing. I stop myself on the verge of spilling my insides, new heart and all, out in front of a woman with whom I've never exchanged more than a dozen words. So I turn back to Lulu, to her squat, red and chrome presence. I push the steel milk pitcher under a wand, turn the knob and let the sound of the steam from Lulu boiling through the milk calm me. I pour the espresso into the bottom of a glass mug, fill it with hot milk and watch the black swirl of espresso slide up the inside of the mug and fade to brown as I top it off with a cloud of foam.

 Something doesn't feel right. I reach down with my right hand and put my fingers on the vein of my left wrist to take my pulse. Its rhythm has changed. It's sharper and faster than it should be, an insistent rapping from inside my arms and legs and at the backs of my hands. I glance at Mila's latte. A dark stain has formed on its surface. On the café's door, the blue lizard is smiling. It's waiting for me to turn and face Mila, waiting to see what my next move will be. My heart beats faster. There's so much to figure out. I suddenly realize that the tiny woman with the scratchy voice forgot to wake me this morning.

 Jonathan Ball

In Vitro City

in vitro city, twenty-two lakes. in vitro city drowning is a way of life. in vitro city we hold hands holding heads under. in vitro city nuclear devices are being re-commissioned. in vitro city, a last resort. in vitro city the walls are glass. in vitro city all things are windows, so there are no windows.

glass is an industry. glass includes reamy, baroque, waterglass, and other textures. glass includes ring mottles, fracture and streamers, drapery, granite, and herringbone ripples. glass nipples. glass making in the area. glass fibre for non-woven and textile applications. glass physics. glass service. glass museums. glass ceilings. glass ground.

bombs are being dropped. bombs at the box office. bombs rising on the market. clustering. bombs in your father's land. by your father's hand. misnamed. erasers at the end of penises.

Lost (a found poem)

Humanoid—sasquatchian ape—rental mask.

   Lovers of these beasts.

   Driving backwards. Very fast.

   Robots. And little robots encased in sac—more lovers.

A man. His wife, driving a truck filled with

   open kerosene barrels—truck stuck—man

   throws lit matches to explode wife.

Prison—tough guys. Resignation to imprisonment.

   Male-female relations explored thru, males

   as normally visualized, females as apes, robots??

       (Overrides hatred unto death.)

Stefanie Freele
Over The Rolling Waters Go

A mother gets hold of some sleeping pills. Four blue capsules nestled in her pinkish palm. The blue just a shade darker than the color they painted their first son's room.

Sleep has not been experienced since the second trimester of her first pregnancy when the acid reflux was so sharp she spent months sitting up in bed far above her sunken and snoozing husband. She stayed alert of course through breastfeeding, barely dozed in between diaper changes, had perpetual insomnia throughout pregnancy number two and with the arrival of the fourth child, she just gave up.

For seven years she has been awake and now with a nest of robin-egg blue pills – oh how innocent they are – she sees a possibility.

Before her husband, who has the kids in the other room doing their pre-dinner stretches, can stop her, she swallows the handful.

She serves her family a tuna noodle casserole, complete with a decoration of potato-chip sailboats. During the coconut cream pie she yawns.

Her husband, holding his puffy bite in mid-air, a dangerous move to do around young children, clears his dad-throat, *honey? That wasn't a yawn was it?*

Guess I must be getting tired after all. She picks at her pie, refusing to look him in the eye.

No time for that hon. He shakes her shoulder. *Right team?*

Go Mom, Go Mom, Go Mom, comes the cheer and for a minute she is revived.

What did Lombardi say? Dad roughs up the hair of the youngest child.

The strength of a group is in the strength of the leaders. Except it comes out as "weaders" and Mom can't help but smile.

Guess I'll go take a shower. She says, knowing how weak and sheepish it sounds, still not looking at any of the lively children around the table, almost ignoring her husband who now drops the fork to the plate.

You took one last week. He gives her that look, the one that always precedes a comment about being the weakest link.

The kids wrestle around on their bench, one muffing up the cap of another, all giggling, until Dad blows his whistle. *Foul! Everyone on dishes.*

The squad sweeps through the kitchen, whisking it clean, shining the sink, lining the washer, pressing buttons. Her husband sits across the table from her and takes her hands in his. *Either you're with us...*

I'm not against you. Another yawn escapes.

Fine then. He lets go of her hands. *Fine. Take your shower.* He pushes away from the table. *Kids. Hup! Hup! Outside.*

Even with the water running she can hear the football game outside in the yard, the oldest is assigning positions, another has ideas for the play, everyone talking at once.

Outside the bathroom door her husband is saying something about *pulling her weight, forging ahead, watching each other's backs.*

If you are talking to me, I can't hear you. The water is tropical-warm like their honeymoon ocean, a memory that now seems lifetimes ago. *Be out soon.* Her eyes are heavy, heavy. The soap is slip slip slippery-

There is a part of her that notices the water getting colder, the strong arms lifting her from the floor, the towel pressed and swiped across her body. Bits of dialogue whisk into her consciousness, *she's on a timeout...dropped the ball...we're not stopping the clock...keep her in the play.*

Her awareness tries to swim out, open her eyes and protest when she hears a child ask if there will be a mom-replacement. *Anyone on bench*, he asks?

But, when her husband responds there won't be any of that, he isn't calling it a rainy day, the collective family cheer of *push on, push on, focus on the trophy* lulls her back to a cozy place.

Since she hasn't slept in seven years, her body twitches, used to morning calisthenics, daily vacuuming, volleyball, soccer, *grab that pigskin and go!*

Finally, with one last harrumph, her groggy mind allows a final husband-missive to get through – *there will be no snivelers on my field* – and then her perception shuts a behemoth door to allow her some rest.

Everything eases toward the color blue.

She drifts over an ocean, a cooler ocean than the honeymoon, this one is a dimmed periwinkle shade, a lovely, inviting sea. Tiny sailboats glide below.

Her body rests on a cottony bed in a corner window with curtains billowing. A cup of tea steams next to her. Smells like jasmine. There is a tiny pitcher of milk, a tiny silver pitcher of honey.

The sea rumbles warmly. The cumulus clouds soar. She sips the tea, reads a good book, another good book – one of kismet and action and compelling character - takes a long bath in the claw foot bathtub on the other side of the room near a window viewing a tumbling river.

Dinner has arrived on a small table lit by candles. Duck, rice, a side salad. Vinaigrette.

On the massage table she melts, rhythms like waves wander back and forth on her scalp. Her feet are held, blanketed, and tucked in.

She sleeps.
And sleeps.

And sleeps.

When she wakes, she is in the same living room where she gave birth four times. The children are in matching sleeping bags rayed away from her like the legs of a starfish. Her husband, ray number five, snores the snore of a horse. All are in uniform, all are wearing war paint.

There are new posters, much like the ones the family makes for the myriad of big games, but these signs say things like *Stand Steady, Stand Strong, She's Our Mom* and *Sleep Is Not De-feet* complete with painted little footprints. Paper plates with half eaten hot dogs have been pushed against the wall. In between the children lay bags of spilled popcorn, soda cans, cheese pretzels, wads of cotton candy.

No one is up yet. No one has seen her. No one moves.

Crawling as silent as she has ever crawled in her life, quieter than most humans possibly can, and like a soldier tiptoeing through a minefield, she eases herself out of the room.

The village-size barrel of Gatorade takes up most of the kitchen counter. Its yellow plastic glows in the early morning light like an extra sun. She finds that she doesn't even need coffee this morning, she is so rested, a pleasure she hasn't experienced in eons.

Even though the moment is peaceful, the house quiet, the birds cheeping their cheeps, there is no hubbub, no chasing, no egging-on.

Using careful strokes, she smears on some of the face-paint left on the counter, starting with sky-blue around the eyes, black stripes down her cheekbones.

Possessing the strength of a hundred mothers, she flexes her arm muscles, circles her shoulders, and inhales as much as oxygen as her lungs will take. Taking care not to step on anyone, she leaps into the living room with the yell of a revolutionary, *I'M UP!*, calling her tribe out for battle, for play, for challenge. She is fierce; she is ready.

LAWRENCE RAAB

SUNRISE WITH SEA MONSTERS
after J.M.W. Turner

There they are, surprisingly pink,
although the rising sun may contribute
to that effect. We who live here
still guess at their actual colors,
their size, even their shape. We've seen them
only as you see them now, lifting
their backs above the ocean, then the edge
of what must be a tail, and their eyes,
unusually large and round and expressionless.
Are they playing? Is it time for them to mate?
We just have to wonder, calling them monsters
because no one's given them a better name.
And because they frighten us, as monsters should.
But you saw them quite clearly, didn't you?
Later, back home, maybe you'll decide
it was a trick of the light, and you'll say
I was the one who persuaded you
they were real. But why would I do that?
I just bring people out here to the cliffs
where they see what they see, and later believe
whatever fits the stories they want to tell.
There they are, farther off. A few more minutes

and the ocean will return to its usual self,
with only a dolphin or two for excitement.
Some say we should kill them,
while others would build them a shrine.
What I know is—they appear, let us look,
and are gone. Or else it's all
just the light, the rising sun like an eye
—the eye of God, I once heard a man say—
staring right through us, burning away
everything we thought we knew.

TESTAMENT

In my youth I wondered often about the past—
how it would change, and where it would end.
Now I can tell you many strange things
will never be revealed, and you
should be glad to understand this.
When I vowed to discover the truth
I tried not to care about being believed.
I walked alone under the wild moon,
listened to the rain unfolding
its many propositions. Those were the days
of certainty and surmise. Thank you
for reading this far. I won't ask
for much more. Perhaps you've found
these pages by chance, and you're hoping
for the wisdom that endings
so often promise. Let me say: assume
nothing about this world, neither
its rules, nor any of its daily habits.
Nor how easily a man can forget
why he threw his life away. Or if,
in fact, I did. I won't excuse myself,
not now. The light that keeps the sky
in place is fading, but it's always fading.
Forget the past if you can. It's never over.
And then it is.

Contributor Notes

Aaron Anstett's collections are *Sustenance*, *No Accideent* (the Nebraska Book Award and the Balcones Prize), and *Each Place the Body's*. He served as the inaugural Pikes Peak Poet Laureate and hopes to inflict another book on the world soon.

Jonathan Ball is the author of two books of poetry: *Ex Machina* (BookThug, 2009) and *Clockfire* (Coach House Books, 2010). He holds a Ph.D. from the University of Calgary, with focuses in Canadian Literature and Creative Writing. His short film *Spoony B* appeared on The Comedy Network, and his screenplay *Way of the Samurai* (co-written with David Navratil) was rewritten and directed by Joseph Novak as the independent feature film *Snake River*. He is the former Managing Editor of *Dandelion* magazine, the former film/video section editor at *Filling Station*, and the former short films programmer for the Gimli Film Festival. He writes the humour column Haiku Horoscopes. Visit him online at www.jonathanball.com.

Electroacoustic composer **Michael Chocholak** was born in New Jersey in 1951. He wrote his first composition on piano at four, and brought himself up between the ululations of short wave radio and the wailings of electric guitar, until he realized that anything was a potential instrument and began writing music based on the holistic world of sound. He has composed for film, video, graphics, dance, theatre, literature, poetry, as well as studio and live performance. His music is on CD from Triple Bath, Howski Industries, Small Doses and Echomusic and freely available on the web. He lives in Eastern Oregon with his wife, writer Misha Nogha, and together they raise Norwegian Fjord horses on their farm, Badger Sett.

Nothing is known about **Richard Crow**. Jonathan Ball is the guardian of the Crow archives.

Brian Evenson is the author of ten books of fiction, most recently *Fugue State*. His other work includes *Last Days*, which was the recipient of the ALA/RUSA award for Best Horror Novel of 2009. A new novel, *Immobility*, is forthcoming in 2012 from Tor. He lives in Providence, Rhode Island and chairs Brown University's Creative Writing Program. www.brianevenson.com

Eliot Fintushel is a writer and performance artist. He began his performance career doing standup comedy at convocations of the Rochester Zen Center and was subsequently persuaded to become a mime. He is the author of numerous short stories and of the novel *Breakfast With The Ones You Love*. Eliot continues to perform solo works in theatres, schools, libraries, and community centers, and is a member of the Imaginists Theater Collective in Santa Rosa, California. He is the father of San Francisco poet Ariel Fintushel. www.fintushel.com

Stefanie Freele is the author of the short story collection *Feeding Strays* (Lost Horse Press), a finalist in the John Gardner Binghamton University Fiction Award and the Book of the Year Award. She recently won the Glimmer Train Fiction Open Award. Her collection, *While Surrounded by Water*, is forthcoming from Press 53 in 2012. Her published and forthcoming fiction can be found in *Glimmer Train*, *American Literary Review*, *Night Train*, *The Florida Review*, *Whitefish Review*, *Necessary Fiction*, *Smokelong Quarterly*, *Pank* and *Corium Magazine*. Stefanie is the Fiction Editor of the *Los Angeles Review*. www.stefaniefreele.com

Wade German is an Canadian-American writer who has been living in Europe since 2001. His poems have been nominated for the Pushcart Prize and the Rhysling Award, and have appeared widely in the U.S. small press and in Australian, Canadian, New Zealand and UK publications. His work has also received honorable mention in Ellen Datlow's *Best Horror of the Year, Volume 2*. He works in broadcast journalism, writing international news.

Carolyn Ives Gilman's first novel, *Halfway Human*, was called "one of the most compelling explorations of gender and power in recent SF" by *Locus* magazine. Her second, *Isles of the Forsaken*, came out in August 2011. Her short fiction has appeared in *Fantasy and Science Fiction, The Year's Best Science Fiction, Bending the Landscape, Interzone, Universe, Full Spectrum*, and *Realms of Fantasy*. She has twice been a finalist for the Nebula Award. In her professional career, Gilman is a historian specializing in 18th- and early 19th-century North American history, particularly frontier and Native history. She lives in St. Louis and works for the Missouri History Museum as a historian and curator.

Daniel Grandbois is the award-winning author of the story collection *Unlucky Lucky Days* (BOA Editions, 2008); the art novel *The Hermaphrodite: An Hallucinated Memoir* (Green Integer, 2010), illustrated by Alfredo Benavidez Bedoya; and the omnibus collection *Unlucky Lucky Tales* (forthcoming 2012, Texas Tech University Press), illustrated by Fidel Sclavo. His work appears in many journals and anthologies, including *Conjunctions, Boulevard, Mississippi Review*, and *Fiction*. As well, he plays in three of the pioneering bands of The Denver Sound: Slim Cessna's Auto Club, Tarantella, and Munly.
www.brothersgrandbois.com

Peter Grandbois is the Barnes and Noble "Discover Great New Writers" and Borders' "Original Voices" author of *The Gravedigger, The Arsenic Lobster: A Hybrid Memoir,* and *Nahoonkara*. His short stories have appeared in journals such as: *Boulevard, The Mississippi Review, Post Road, New Orleans Review, Gargoyle,* and *The Denver Quarterly*. His work has been shortlisted for a Pushcart Prize and nominated for the National Book Award. He teaches at Denison University in Ohio and can be reached at
www.brothersgrandbois.com

Thomas E. Kennedy's 25+ books include the novels *Falling Sideways (*Bloomsbury *2011)* and *In the Company of Angels* (Bloomsbury 2010), which was chosen by Jonathan Yardley in *The Washington Post* as his favorite novel of that year. Yardley also wrote that "*Falling Sideways* is that rarest of commodities in American literary fiction, a novel about men and women at work; it is part-satire and part-drama, and it is very smart." In 2012 New American Press will publish his *New & Selected Stories, 1982-2012*.
www.thomasekennedy.com

Joshua McKinney is the author of two books of poetry: *Saunter*, co-winner of the University of Georgia Press Open Competition and *The Novice Mourner*, recipient of the Dorothy Brunsman Poetry Prize from Bear Star Press. His recent work appears in the current or forthcoming issues of *New American Writing, New Ohio Review, Colorado Review, Denver Quarterly, Ping Pong, VOLT*, and other journals. He teaches literature and creative writing at California State University, Sacramento. More about Joshua at:
www.joshuamckinneypoet.com

Joe L. Murr has lived on every continent except Antarctica. He currently divides his time between Finland and the Netherlands. His fiction has been published in *Beneath Ceaseless Skies*, *ChiZine*, *Dark Recesses*, and other publications.

Jessica Plattner is an Oregon artist and educator whose work has been exhibited in the United States, Mexico, Canada, and Italy. She is currently on sabbatical from Eastern Oregon University, and is serving as Visiting Artist-in-residence at Medicine Hat College in Alberta, Canada, and Studio Art Centers International (SACI) in Florence, Italy. The new body of work created during her sabbatical will be exhibited at the Pendleton Center for the Arts in Pendleton, Oregon, in October 2012. She lives with her partner, artist-musician Dean Smale and their baby daughter Sofonisba.

Lawrence Raab is the author of seven collections of poems, including *What We Don't Know About Each Other* (winner of the National Poetry Series, and a Finalist for the National Book Award), *The Probable World*, and *Visible Signs: New and Selected Poems,* all published by Penguin. His latest collection is *The History of Forgetting* (Penguin, 2009). He teaches literature and writing at Williams College.

Nisi Shawl's *Filter House* (Aqueduct Press, 2008) won the 2009 James Tiptree, Jr. Award and was nominated for the World Fantasy Award. Shawl is one of the founders of the Carl Brandon Society, and co-author, with Cynthia Ward, of *Writing the Other: a Practical Approach*. She edited *WisCon Chronicles 5: Writing and Racial Identity*. *Something More and More*, a collection celebrating her WisCon 35 Guest of Honor status, appeared in May 2011 from Aqueduct Press. Her poem "Transbluency" appeared in the June/July issue of *Stone Telling*. Shawl is an alumna of the Clarion West Writers Workshop and serves on its Board of Directors.

Anita Sullivan has two poetry collections, *The Middle Window* (a chapbook from Traprock Books, 2008), and *Garden of Beasts* (Airlie Press, 2010). She has published essays and poems in a variety of journals, and holds an MFA in poetry from Pacific Lutheran University. She lives in Eugene, Oregon.

Geronimo G. Tagatac's fiction has appeared in journals and anthologies, including, *Orion*, *Alternatives Magazine*, *The Northwest Review*, *Best Writing of the American West* and *Tilting the Continent, Growing Up Filipino II*. He's been the recipient of an Oregon Literary Arts Fellowship. His short fiction collection, *The Weight of the Sun*, was nominated for an Oregon Book Award. Geronimo lives and writes in Salem, Oregon.

David Eric Tomlinson is a writer who has an unhealthy relationship with caffeine. He can usually be found in the coffee shops of north Dallas, USA, furiously finishing his first novel. "The Ornithologist's Last Wish" is David's first published short story. You can read more of his work online at www.DavidEricTomlinson.com

Jodi Varon is the author of *Drawing to an Inside Straight: The Legacy of an Absent Father* and *The Rock's Cold Breath: Selected Poems of Li He*, translations from the Chinese. Her most recent work appears in *Texas Told 'Em: Gambling Stories* and *WomenArts Quarterly Journal*. An interpreter of the contributions of Chinese Americans in eastern Oregon, she also writes for the *Oregon Encyclopedia*. She is a professor of English at Eastern Oregon University.

Ray Vukcevich's latest book is *Boarding Instructions* from Fairwood Press. His other books are *Meet Me in the Moon Room* from Small Beer Press and *The Man of Maybe Half-a-Dozen Faces* from St. Martin's. His short fiction has appeared in many magazines and anthologies. Read more about him at
ww.rayvuk.com

ACKNOWLEDGMENTS

"Good Morning," by Aaron Anstett was published in his collection, *No Accident,* which was selected by Philip Levine for the Backwaters Press Prize and published by Backwaters Press in 2005. In 2006 it won both the Nebraska Book Award in Poetry and the Balcones Poetry Prize. Reprinted with permission of the author.

"Rabbit" and "Moon" by Stephen McNally are reprinted from *Child in Amber*. Copyright © 1993 by Stephen McNally and published by the University of Massachusetts Press. Reprinted with permission from the publisher.

"Jars" by Brian Evenson is reprinted by his collection, *The Din of Celestial Birds*, Copyright © 1997, Brian Evenson, published by Wordcraft of Oregon. Reprinted with permission of the author.

"Realism & Other Illusions," by Thomas E. Kennedy, is reprinted from the collection of essays by the same name. Copyright © 2002, Thomas E. Kennedy. Published by Wordcraft of Oregon. The essay was selected by *The Best Writing on Writing*, Vol. Two (Cincinatti, Ohio: Story Press, 1995).

four great short story collections for readers who like to let their imaginations drift

After the Apocalypse: Stories
Maureen F. McHugh
$16 · 978-1-931520-29-4 · OCTOBER 2011

★ "Nine fierce, wry, stark, beautiful stories. . . . But there is no suicidal drama, and the overall effect is optimistic: we may wreck our planet, our economies, and our bodies, but every apocalypse will have an "after" in which people find their own peculiar ways of getting by."
—*Publishers Weekly* (starred review)

Three Messages and a Warning:
Contemporary Mexican Short Stories of the Fantastic
Eduardo Jimenez Mayo & Chris N. Brown, eds.
$16 · 978-1-931520-31-7 · DECEMBER 2011

"Langorous, edgy, sumptuously beautiful by turns, *Three Messages* expands our understanding of contemporary Mexican literary production, collapsing high-low boundaries and pre-established ideas about national identity."
—Debra Castillo, Emerson Hinchliff
Professor of Spanish Literature, Cornell University

Paradise Tales
Geoff Ryman
$16 · 978-1-931520-44-7

★ "Often contemplative and subtly ironic, the 16 stories in this outstanding collection work imaginative riffs on a variety of fantasy and SF themes. . . . Readers of all stripes will appreciate these thoughtful tales."
—*Publishers Weekly* (Starred Review)

The Monkey's Wedding and Other Stories
Joan Aiken
$24 · 978-1-931520-74-4

★ "Wildly inventive, darkly lyrical, and always surprising. . . a literary treasure that should be cherished by fantastical fiction fans of all ages."
—*Publishers Weekly*
(starred review)

Distributed to the trade by Consortium.
smallbeerpress.com · facebook.com/smallbeerpress · weightlessbooks.com

clarion

June 24 – August 4
at the University of California, San Diego

Writers-in-Residence

Jeffrey Ford
Marjorie Liu
Ted Chiang
Walter Jon Williams
Holly Black
Cassie Clare

apply at: http://clarion.ucsd.edu
Deadline: March 1, 2012

See you in San Diego

Did you know that natural redheads make up only 4% of the population?

With that in mind, why not entrust your graphic design needs to someone who truly understands what it is to be rare, intriguing and memorable?

specializing in print: book covers · CD covers · logos · catalogs · wine labels · ads · posters · and more!

redbat design

the hair is red...the mind unique

kristin summers
graphic designer

541/962-7176
la grande, oregon
kj@redbatdesign.com

www.redbatdesign.com

Submissions Open for Issue No. 2
December 1, 2011 to March 31, 2012

Flash Fiction and Short Essays up to 2000 words, pays $25
Short Stories, 2001 - 6500 words, pays $50
Features and Interviews, 2001 - 5000 words, pays $50
Poems up to 96 lines, pays $10

Submit on-line by following link at:

www.wordcraftoforegon.com/pd.html

CPSIA information can be obtained at www.ICGtesting.com
Printed in the USA
LVOW11s1434070913

351427LV00008B/694/P